THE PROBLEM OF INCREASING HUMAN ENERGY

THE PROBLEM OF INCREASING HUMAN ENERGY

(1900)

WITH SPECIAL REFERENCE TO THE HARNESSING OF THE SUN'S ENERGY.

BY

Nikola Tesla

KALPAZ

ISBN: 978-93-5128-556-4

First Published in 1900
Indian Reprint in 2017

Published by

Kalpaz Publications
C-30, Satyawati Nagar,
Delhi – 110052
E-mail: kalpaz@hotmail.com
Website: kalpazpublications.com
Ph.: +91-9212142040

Cataloging in Publication Data—DK
Courtesy: D.K. Agencies (P) Ltd. <docinfo@dkagencies.com>

Tesla, Nikola, 1856-1943, **author.**
The problem of increasing human energy (1900) : with special reference to the harnessing of the sun's energy / by Nikola Tesla.
pages cm
"First published in 1900"—Title page verso.
ISBN 9789351285564

1. Power resources. 2. Force and energy. 3. Human physiology. 4. Electric power transmission. 5. Tesla, Nikola, 1856-1943. I. Title.

TJ163.24.T47 2017 DDC 333.79 23

THE PROBLEM OF INCREASING HUMAN ENERGY

THE ONWARD MOVEMENT OF MAN—THE ENERGY OF THE MOVEMENT—THE THREE WAYS OF INCREASING HUMAN ENERGY.

Of all the endless variety of phenomena which nature presents to our senses, there is none that fills our minds with greater wonder than that inconceivably complex movement which, in its entirety, we designate as human life; Its mysterious origin is veiled in the forever impenetrable mist of the past, its character is rendered incomprehensible by its infinite intricacy, and its destination is hidden in the unfathomable depths of the future. Whence does it come? What is it? Whither does it tend? are the great questions which the sages of all times have endeavored to answer.

Modern science says: The sun is the past, the earth is the present, the moon is the future. From an incandescent mass we have originated, and into a frozen mass we shall turn. Merciless is the law of nature, and rapidly and irresistibly we are drawn to our doom. Lord Kelvin, in his profound meditations, allows us only a short span of life, something like six million years, after which time the suns bright light will have ceased to shine, and its life giving heat will have ebbed away, and our own earth will be a lump of ice, hurrying on through the eternal night. But do not let us despair. There will still be left upon it a glimmering spark of life, and there will be a chance to kindle a new fire on some distant star. This wonderful possibility seems, indeed, to exist, judging from Professor Dewar's beautiful experiments with liquid air, which show that germs of organic life are not destroyed by cold, no matter how intense; consequently they may be transmitted through the interstellar space. Meanwhile the cheering lights of science and art, ever increasing in intensity, illuminate our path, and marvels they disclose, and the enjoyments they offer, make us measurably forgetful of the gloomy future.

Though we may never be able to comprehend human life, we know certainly that it is a movement, of whatever nature it be. The existence of movement unavoidably implies a body which is being moved and a force which is moving it. Hence, wherever there is life, there is a mass moved by a force. All mass possesses inertia, all force tends to persist. Owing to this universal property and condition, a body, be it at rest or in motion, tends to remain in the same state, and a force, manifesting itself anywhere and through whatever cause, produces an equivalent opposing force, and as an absolute necessity of this it follows that every movement in nature must be rhythmical. Long ago this simple truth was clearly pointed out by Herbert Spencer, who

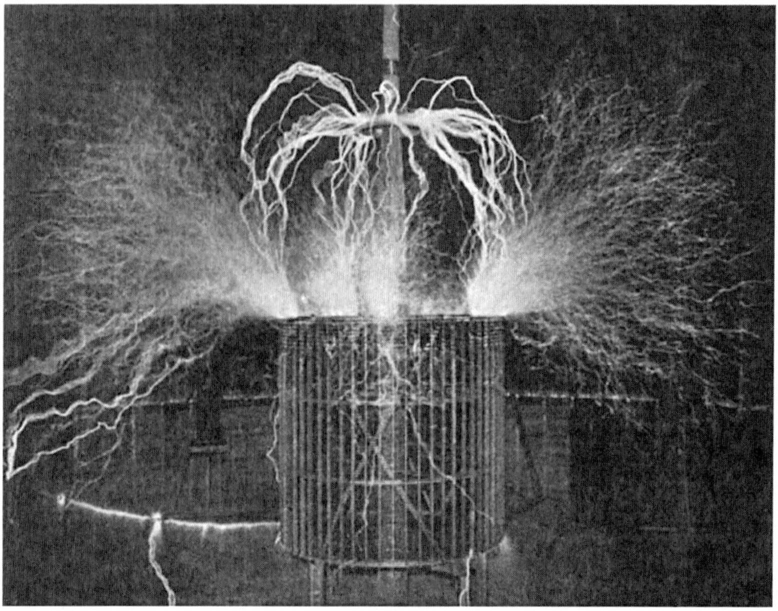

FIG. 1. BURNING THE NITROGEN OF THE ATMOSPHERE.

Note to Fig. 1.—This result is produced by the discharge of an electrical oscillator giving twelve million volts. The electrical pressure, alternating one hundred thousand times per second, excites the normally inert nitrogen, causing it to combine with the oxygen. The flame-like discharge shown in the photograph measures sixty-five feet across.

arrived at it through a somewhat different process of reasoning. It is borne out in everything we perceive—in the movement of a planet, in the surging and ebbing of the tide, in the reverberations of the air, the swinging of a pendulum, the oscillations of an electric current, and in the infinitely varied phenomena of organic life. Does not the whole of human life attest to it? Birth, growth, old age, and death of an individual, family, race, or nation, what is it all but a rhythm? All life-manifestation, then, even in its most intricate form, as exemplified in man, however involved and inscrutable, is only a movement, to which the same general laws of movement which govern throughout the physical universe must be applicable.

When we speak of man, we have a conception of humanity as a whole, and before applying scientific methods to, the investigation of his movement we must accept this as a physical fact. But can anyone doubt to-day that all the millions of individuals and all the innumerable types and characters constitute an entity, a unit? Though free to think and act, we are held together, like the stars in the firmament, with ties inseparable. These ties cannot be seen, but we can feel them. I cut myself in the finger, and it pains me: this finger is a part of me. I see a friend hurt, and it hurts me, too: my friend and I are one. And now I see stricken down an enemy, a lump of matter which, of all the lumps of matter in the universe, I care least for, and it still grieves me. Does this not prove that each of us is only part of a whole?

For ages this idea has been proclaimed in the consummately wise teachings of religion, probably not alone as a means of insuring peace and harmony among men, but as a deeply founded truth. The Buddhist expresses it in one way, the Christian in another, but both say the same: We are all one. Metaphysical proofs are, however, not the only ones which we are able to bring forth in support of this idea. Science, too, recognizes this connectedness of separate individuals, though not quite in the same sense as it admits that the suns, planets, and moons of a constellation are one body, and there can be no doubt that it will be experimentally confirmed in times to come, when our means and methods for investigating psychical and other states and phenomena shall have been brought to great perfection. Still more: this one human being lives on and on. The individual is ephemeral, races and nations come and pass away, but man remains. Therein lies the profound difference between the individual and the whole. Therein, too, is to be found the partial explanation of many of those marvelous phenomena of heredity which are the result of countless centuries of feeble but persistent influence.

Conceive, then, man as a mass urged on by a force. Though this movement is not of a translatory character, implying change of place, yet the general laws of mechanical movement are applicable to it, and the energy associated with this mass can be measured, in accordance with well-known principles, by half the product of the mass with the square of a certain velocity. So, for instance, a cannon-ball which is at rest possesses a certain amount of energy in the form of heat, which we measure in a similar way. We imagine the ball to consist of innumerable minute particles, called atoms or molecules, which vibrate or whirl around one another. We determine their masses and velocities, and from them the energy of each of these minute systems, and adding them all together, we get an idea of the total heat-energy contained in the ball, which is only seemingly at rest. In this purely theoretical estimate this energy may then be calculated by multiplying half of the total mass–that is half of the sum of all the small masses–with the square of a velocity which is determined from the velocities of the separate particles. In like manner we may conceive of human energy being measured by half the human mass multiplied with the square of the velocity which we are not yet able to compute. But our deficiency in this knowledge will not vitiate the truth of the deductions I shall draw, which rest on the firm basis that the same laws of mass and force govern throughout nature.

Man, however, is not an ordinary mass, consisting of spinning atoms and molecules, and containing merely heat-energy. He is a mass possessed of certain higher qualities by reason of the creative principle of life with which he is endowed. His mass, as the water in an ocean wave, is being continuously exchanged, new taking the place of the old. Not only this, but he grows propagates, and dies, thus altering his mass independently, both in bulk and density. What is most wonderful of all, he is capable of increasing or diminishing his velocity of movement by the mysterious power he possesses by appropriating more or less energy from other substance, and turning it into motive energy. But in any given moment we may ignore these slow changes and assume that human energy is measured by half the product of man's mass with the square of a certain hypothetical velocity. However we may compute this velocity, and whatever we may take as the standard of its measure, we must, in harmony with this conception, come to the conclusion that the great problem of science is, and always will be, to increase the energy thus defined. Many years ago, stimulated by the perusal of that deeply interesting work, Draper's "History of the Intellectual Development of Europe," depicting so vividly human movement, I recognized that to solve this eternal problem must ever be the chief task of the man of science. Some results of my own efforts to this end I shall endeavor briefly to describe here.

Let, then, in diagram *a*, *M* represent the mass of man. This mass is impelled in one direction by a force *f*, which is resisted by another partly frictional and partly negative force *R*, acting in a direction exactly opposite, and retarding the movement of the mass. Such an antagonistic force is present in every movement and must be taken into consideration. The difference between these two forces is the effective force which imparts a velocity *V* to the mass *M* in the direction of the arrow on the line representing the force *f*. In accordance with the preceding, the human energy will then be given by the product $\frac{1}{2} MV^2 = -\frac{1}{2} MV \times V$, in which *M* is the total mass of man in the ordinary interpretation of the term "mass," and *V* is a certain hypothetical velocity, which, in the present state of science, we are unable exactly to define and determine. To increase the human energy is, therefore, equivalent to increasing this product, and there are, as will readily be seen, only three ways possible to attain this result, which are illustrated in the above diagram. The first way shown in the top figure, is to increase the mass (as indicated by the dotted circle), leaving the two opposing forces the same. The second way is to reduce the retarding force *R* to a smaller value *r*, leaving the mass and the impelling force the same, as diagrammatically shown in the middle figure. The third way, which is illustrated in the last figure, is to increase the impelling force *f* to a higher value *F*, while the mass and the retarding force *R* remain unaltered. Evidently fixed limits exist as regards increase of mass and reduction of retarding force, but the impelling force can be increased indefinitely. Each

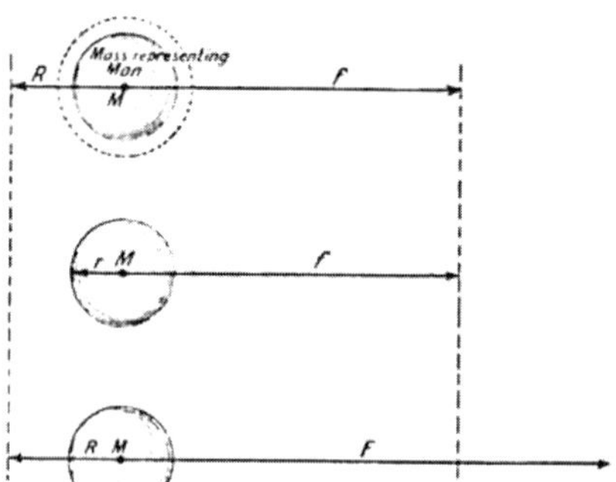

DIAGRAM a. *THE THREE WAYS OF INCREASING HUMAN ENERGY.*

of these three possible solutions presents a different aspect of the main problem of increasing human energy, which is thus divided into three distinct problems, to be successively considered.

THE FIRST PROBLEM: HOW TO INCREASE THE HUMAN MASS—THE BURNING OF ATMOSPHERIC NITROGEN

Viewed generally, there are obviously two ways of increasing the mass of mankind: first, by aiding and maintaining those forces and conditions which tend to increase it; and, second, by opposing and reducing those which tend to diminish it. The mass will be increased by careful attention to health, by substantial food, by moderation, by regularity of habits, by promotion of marriage, by conscientious attention to children, and, generally stated, by the observance of all the many precepts and laws of religion and hygiene. But in adding new mass to the old, three cases again present themselves. Either the mass added is of the same velocity as the old, or it is of a smaller or of a higher velocity. To gain an idea of the relative importance of these cases, imagine a train composed of, say, one hundred locomotives running on a track, and suppose that, to increase the energy of the moving mass, four more locomotives are added to the train. If these four move at the same velocity at which the train is going, the total energy will be increased four per cent.; if they are moving at only one half of that velocity, the increase will amount to only one per cent.; if they are moving at twice that velocity, the increase of energy will be sixteen per cent. This simple illustration shows that it is of greatest importance to add mass of a higher velocity. Stated more to the point, if, for example, the children be of the same degree of enlightenment as the parents,–that is, mass of the "same velocity,"–the energy will simply increase proportionately to the number added. If they are less intelligent or advanced, or mass of "smaller velocity," there will be a very slight gain in the energy; but if they are further advanced, or mass of "higher velocity," then the new generation will add very considerably to the sum total of human energy. any addition of mass of "smaller velocity," beyond that indispensable amount required by the law expressed in the proverb, "Mens sana in corpore sano," should be strenuously opposed. For instance, the mere development of muscle, as aimed at in some of our colleges, I consider equivalent to adding mass of "smaller velocity," and I would not commend it, although my views were different when I was a student myself. Moderate exercise, insuring the right balance between mind and body, and the highest efficiency of performance, is, of course, a prime requirement. The above example shows that the most important result to be attained is the education, or the increase of the "velocity," of the mass newly added.

Conversely, it scarcely need be stated that everything that is against the teachings of religion and the laws of hygiene is tending to decrease the mass. Whisky, wine, tea coffee, tobacco, and other such stimulants are responsible for the shortening of the lives of many, and ought to be used with moderation. But I do not think that rigorous measures of suppression of habits followed through many generations are commendable. It is wiser to preach moderation than abstinence. We have become accustomed to these stimulants, and if such reforms are to be effected, they must be slow and gradual. Those who are devoting their energies to such ends could make themselves far more useful by turning their efforts in other directions, as, for instance, toward providing pure water.

For every person who perishes from the effects of a stimulant, at least a thousand die from the consequences of drinking impure water. This precious fluid, which daily infuses new life into us, is likewise the chief vehicle through which disease and death enter our bodies. The germs of destruction it conveys are enemies all the more terrible as they perform their fatal work unperceived. They seal our doom while we live and enjoy. The majority of people are so ignorant or careless in drinking water, and the consequences of this are so disastrous, that a philanthropist can scarcely use his efforts better than by endeavoring to enlighten those who are thus injuring themselves. By systematic purification and sterilization of the drinking water the human mass would be very considerably increased. It should be made a rigid rule—which might be enforced by law—to boil or to sterilize otherwise the drinking water in every household and public place. The mere filtering does not afford sufficient security against infection. All ice for internal uses should be artificially prepared from water thoroughly sterilized. The importance of eliminating germs of disease from the city water is generally recognized, but little is being done to improve the existing conditions, as no satisfactory method of sterilizing great quantities of water has yet been brought forward. By improved electrical appliances we are now enabled to produce ozone cheaply and in large amounts, and this ideal disinfectant seems to offer a happy solution of the important question.

Gambling, business rush, and excitement, particularly on the exchanges, are causes of much mass reduction, all the more so because the individuals concerned represent units of higher value. Incapacity of observing the first symptoms of an illness, and careless neglect of the same, are important factors of mortality. In noting carefully every new sign of approaching danger, and making conscientiously every possible effort to avert it, we are not only following wise laws of hygiene in the interest of our well-being and the success of our labors, but we are also complying with a higher moral duty. Everyone should consider his body as a priceless gift from one whom he loves above all, as a marvelous work of art, of indescribable beauty and mastery beyond human conception, and so delicate and frail that a word, a breath, a look, nay, a thought, may injure it. Uncleanliness, which breeds disease and death, is not only a self destructive but highly immoral habit. In keeping our bodies free from infection, healthful, and pure, we are expressing our reverence for the high principle with which they are endowed. He who follows the precepts of hygiene in this spirit is proving himself, so far, truly religious. Laxity of morals is a terrible evil, which poisons both mind and body, and which is responsible for a great reduction of the human mass in some countries. Many of the present customs and tendencies are productive of similar hurtful results. For example, the society life, modern education and pursuits of women, tending to draw them away from their household duties and make men out of them, must needs detract from the elevating ideal they represent, diminish the artistic creative power, and cause sterility and a general weakening of the race. A thousand other evils might be mentioned, but all put together, in their bearing upon the problem under discussion, they could not equal a single one, the want of food, brought on by poverty, destitution, and famine. Millions of individuals die yearly for want of food, thus keeping down the mass. Even in our enlightened communities, and not withstanding the many charitable efforts, this is still, in all probability, the chief evil. I do not mean here absolute want of food, but want of healthful nutriment.

How to provide good and plentiful food is, therefore, a most important question of the day. On the general principles the raising of cattle as a means of providing food is objectionable, because, in the sense interpreted above, it must undoubtedly tend to the addition of mass of a "smaller velocity." It is certainly preferable to raise vegetables, and I think, therefore, that vegetarianism is a commendable departure from the established barbarous habit. That we can subsist on plant food and perform our work even to advantage is not a theory, but a well-demonstrated fact. Many races living almost exclusively on vegetables are of superior physique and strength. There is no doubt that some plant food, such as oatmeal, is more economical than meat, and superior to it in regard to both mechanical and mental performance. Such food, moreover, taxes our digestive organs decidedly less, and, in making us more contented and sociable, produces an amount of good difficult to estimate. In view of these facts every effort should be made to stop the wanton and cruel slaughter of animals, which must be destructive to our morals. To free ourselves from animal instincts and appetites, which keep us down, we should begin at the very root from which we spring: we should effect a radical reform in the character of the food.

There seems to be no *philosophical* necessity for food. We can conceive of organized beings living without nourishment, and deriving all the energy they need for the performance of their life functions from the ambient medium. In a crystal we have the clear evidence of the existence of a formative life-principle, and though we cannot understand the life of a crystal, it is none the less a living being. There may be, besides crystals, other such individualized, material systems of beings, perhaps of gaseous constitution, or composed of substance still more tenuous. In view of this possibility,—nay, probability,—we cannot apodictically deny the existence of organized beings on a planet merely because the conditions on the same are unsuitable for the existence of life as we conceive it. We cannot even, with positive assurance, assert that some of them might not be present here, in this our world, in the very midst of us, for their constitution and life-manifestation may be such that we are unable to perceive them.

The production of artificial food as a means for causing an increase of the human mass naturally suggests itself, but a direct attempt of this kind to provide nourishment does not appear to me rational, at least not for the present. Whether we could thrive on such food is very doubtful. We are the result of ages of continuous adaptation, and we cannot radically change without unforeseen and, in all probability, disastrous consequences. So uncertain an experiment should not be tried. By far the best way, it seems to me, to meet the ravages of the evil, would be to find ways of increasing the productivity of the soil. With this object the preservation of forests is of an importance which cannot be overestimated, and in this connection, also, the utilization of water-power for purposes of electrical transmission, dispensing in many ways with the necessity of burning wood, and tending thereby to forest preservation, is to be strongly advocated. But there are limits in the improvement to be effected in this and similar ways.

To increase materially the productivity of the soil, it must be more effectively fertilized by artificial means. The question of food-production resolves itself, then, into the question how best to fertilize the soil. What it is that made the soil is still a mystery. To explain its origin is probably equivalent to explaining the origin of life itself. The rocks, disintegrated by moisture and heat and wind and weather, were in themselves not capable of maintaining life. Some unexplained condition arose, and some new principle came into effect, and the first layer capable of sustaining low organisms, like mosses was formed. These, by their life and death, added more of the life sustaining quality to the soil, and higher organisms could then subsist, and so on and on, until at last highly developed plant and animal life could flourish. But though the theories are, even now, not in agreement as to how fertilization is effected, it is a fact, only too well ascertained, that the soil cannot indefinitely sustain life, and some way must be found to supply it with the substances which have been abstracted from it by the plants. The chief and most valuable among these substances are compounds of nitrogen, and the cheap production of these is, therefore, the key for the solution of the all-important food problem. Our atmosphere contains an inexhaustible amount of nitrogen, and could we but oxidize it and produce these compounds, an incalculable benefit for mankind would follow.

Long ago this idea took a powerful hold on the imagination of scientific men, but an efficient means for accomplishing this result could not be devised. The problem was rendered extremely difficult by the extraordinary inertness of the nitrogen, which refuses to combine even with oxygen. But here electricity comes to our aid: the dormant affinities of the element are awakened by an electric current of the proper quality. As a lump of coal which has been in contact with oxygen for centuries without burning will combine with it when once ignited, so nitrogen, excited by electricity, will burn. I did not succeed, however, in producing electrical discharges exciting very effectively the atmospheric nitrogen until a comparatively recent date, although I showed, in May, 1891, in a scientific lecture, a novel form of discharge or electrical flame named "St. Elmo's hotfire," which, besides being capable of generating ozone in abundance, also possessed, as I pointed out on that occasion, distinctly the quality of exciting chemical affinities. This discharge or flame was then only three or four inches long, its chemical action was likewise very feeble, and consequently the process of oxidation of nitrogen was wasteful. How to intensify this action was the question. Evidently electric currents of a peculiar kind had to be produced in order to render the process of nitrogen combustion more efficient.

The first advance was made in ascertaining that the chemical activity of the discharge was very considerably increased by using currents of extremely high frequency or rate of vibration. This was an important improvement, but practical considerations soon set a definite limit to the progress in this direction. Next, the effects of the electrical pressure of the current impulses, of their wave-form and other characteristic features, were investigated. Then the influence of the atmospheric pressure and temperature and of the presence of water and other bodies was studied, and thus the best conditions for causing the most intense chemical action of the discharge and securing the highest efficiency of the process were gradually ascertained. Naturally, the improvements were not quick in coming; still, little by little, I advanced. The flame grew larger and larger, and its oxidizing action grew more intense. From an insignificant brush-discharge a few inches long it developed into a marvelous electrical phenomenon, a roaring blaze, devouring the nitrogen of the atmosphere and measuring sixty or seventy feet across. Thus slowly, almost imperceptibly, possibility became accomplishment. All is not yet done, by any means, but to what a degree my efforts have been rewarded an idea may be gained from an inspection of Fig. 1 (p. 176), which, with its title, is self explanatory. The flame-like discharge visible is produced by the intanse electrical oscillations which pass through the coil shown, and violently agitate the electrified molecules of the air. By this means a strong affinity is created between the two normally indifferent constituents of the atmosphere, and they combine readily, even if no further provision is made for intensifying the chemical action of the discharge. In the manufacture of nitrogen compounds by this method, of course, every possible means bearing upon the intensity of this action and the efficiency of the process will be taken advantage of, and, besides, special arrangements will be provided for the fixation of the compounds formed, as they are generally unstable, the nitrogen becoming again inert after a little lapse of time. Steam is a simple and effective means for fixing permanently the compounds. The result illustrated makes it practicable to oxidize the atmospheric nitrogen in unlimited quantities, merely by the use of cheap mechanical power and simple electrical apparatus. In this manner many compounds of nitrogen may be manufactured all over the world, at a small cost, and in any desired amount, and by means of these compounds the soil can be fertilized and its productiveness indefinitely increased. An abundance of cheap and healthful food, not artificial, but such as we are accustomed to, may thus be obtained. This new and inexhaustible source of food-supply will be of incalculable benefit to mankind, for it will enormously contribute to the increase of the human mass, and thus add immensely to human energy. Soon, I hope, the world will see the beginning of an industry which, in time to come, will, I believe, be in importance next to that if iron.

THE SECOND PROBLEM: HOW TO REDUCE THE FORCE RETARDING THE HUMAN MASS—THE ART OF TELAUTOMATICS.

As before stated, the force which retards the onward movement of man is partly frictional and partly negative. To illustrate this distinction I may name, for example, ignorance, stupidity, and imbecility as some of the purely frictional forces, or resistances devoid of any directive tendency. On the other hand, visionariness, insanity, self-destructive tendency, religious fanaticism, and the like, are all forces of a negative character, acting in definite directions. To reduce or entirely overcome these dissimilar retarding forces, radically different methods must be employed. One knows, for instance, what a fanatic may do, and one can take preventive measures, can enlighten, convince, and, possibly direct him, turn his vice into virtue; but one does not know, and never can know, what a brute or an imbecile may do, and one must deal with him as with a mass, inert, without mind, let loose by the mad elements. A negative force always implies some quality, not infrequently a high one, though badly directed, which it is possible to turn to good advantage; but a directionless, frictional force involves unavoidable loss. Evidently, then, the first and general answer to the above question is: turn all negative force in the right direction and reduce all frictional force.

There can be no doubt that, of all the frictional resistances, the one that most retards human movement is ignorance. Not without reason said that man of wisdom, Buddha: "Ignorance is the greatest evil in the world." The friction which results from ignorance, and which is greatly increased owing to the numerous languages and nationalities, can be reduced only by the spread of knowledge and the unification of the heterogeneous elements of humanity. No effort could be better spent. But however ignorance may have retarded the onward movement of man in times past, it is certain that, nowadays, negative forces have become of greater importance. Among these there is one of far greater moment than any other. It is called organized warfare. When we consider the millions of individuals, often the ablest in mind and body, the flower of humanity, who are compelled to a life of inactivity and unproductiveness, the immense sums of money daily required for the maintenance of armies and war apparatus, representing ever so much of human energy, all the effort uselessly spent in the production of arms and implements of destruction, the loss of life and the fostering of a barbarous spirit, we are appalled at the inestimable loss to mankind which the existence of these deplorable conditions must involve. What can we do to combat best this great evil?

Law and order absolutely require the maintenance of organized force. No community can exist and prosper without rigid discipline. Every country must be able to defend itself, should the necessity arise. The conditions of to-day are not the result of yesterday, and a radical change cannot be effected to-morrow. If the nations would at once disarm, it is more than likely that a state of things worse than war itself would follow. Universal peace is a beautiful dream, but not at once realizable. We have seen recently that even the nobel effort of the man invested with the greatest worldly power has been virtually without effect. And no wonder, for the establishment of universal peace is, for the time being, a physical impossibility. War is a negative force, and cannot be turned in a positive direction without passing through, the intermediate phases. It is a problem of making a wheel, rotating one way, turn in the opposite direction without slowing it down, stopping it, and speeding it up again the other way.

It has been argued that the perfection of guns of great destructive power will stop warfare. So I myself thought for a long time, but now I believe this to be a profound mistake. Such developments will greatly modify, but not arrest it. On the contrary, I think that every new arm that is invented, every new departure that is made in this direction, merely invites new talent and skill, engages new effort, offers new incentive, and so only gives a fresh impetus to further development. Think of the discovery of gun-powder. Can we conceive of any more radical departure than was effected by this innovation? Let us imagine ourselves living in that period: would we not have thought then that warfare was at an end, when the armor of the knight became an object of ridicule, when bodily strength and skill, meaning so much before, became of comparatively little value? Yet gunpowder did not stop warfare: quite the opposite—it acted as a most powerful incentive. Nor do I believe that warfare can ever be arrested by any scientific or ideal development, so long as similar conditions to those prevailing now exist, because war has itself become a science, and because war involves some of the most sacred sentiments of which man is capable. In fact, it is doubtful whether men who would not be ready to fight for a high principle would be good for anything at all. It is not the mind which makes man, nor is it the body; it is mind and body. Our virtues and our failings are inseparable, like force and matter. When they separate, man is no more.

Another argument, which carries considerable force, is frequently made, namely, that war must soon become impossible be cause the means of defense are outstripping the means of attack. This is only in accordance with a fundamental law which may be expressed by the statement that it is easier to destroy than to build. This law defines human capacities and human conditions.

Were these such that it would be easier build than to destroy, man would go on unresisted, creating and accumulating without limit. Such conditions are not of this earth. A being which could do this would not be a man: it might be a god. Defense will always have the advantage over attack, but this alone, it seems to me, can never stop war. By the use of new principles of defense we can render harbors impregnable against attack, but we cannot by such means prevent two warships meeting in battle on the high sea. And then, if we follow this idea to its ultimate development, we are led to the conclusion that it would be better for mankind if attack and defense were just oppositely related; for if every country, even the smallest, could surround itself with a wall absolutely impenetrable, and could defy the rest of the world, a state of things would surely be brought on which would be extremely unfavorable to human progress. It is by abolishing all the barriers which separate nations and countries that civilization is best furthered.

Again, it is contended by some that the advent of the flying-machine must bring on universal peace. This, too, I believe to be an entirely erroneous view. The flying-machine is certainly coming, and very soon, but the conditions will remain the same as before. In fact, I see no reason why a ruling power, like Great Britain, might not govern the air as well as the sea. Without wishing to put myself on record as a prophet, I do not hesitate to say that the next years will see the establishment of an "air-power," and its center may be not far from New York. But, for all that, men will fight on merrily.

The ideal development of the war principle would ultimately lead to the transformation of the whole energy of war into purely potential, explosive energy, like that of an electrical condenser. In this form the war-energy could be maintained without effort; it would need to be much smaller in amount, while incomparably more effective.

As regards the security of a country against foreign invasion, it is interesting to note that it depends only on the relative, and not the absolute, number of the individuals or magnitude of the forces, and that, if every country should reduce the war-force in the same ratio, the security would remain unaltered. An international agreement with the object of reducing to a minimum the war-force which, in view of the present still imperfect education of the masses, is absolutely indispensable, would, therefore, seem to be the first rational step to take toward diminishing the force retarding human movement.

Fortunately, the existing conditions cannot continue indefinitely, for a new element is beginning to assert itself. A change for the better is eminent, and I shall now endeavor to show what, according to my ideas, will be the first advance toward the establishment of peaceful relations between nations, and by what means it will eventually be accomplished.

Let us go back to the early beginning, when the law of the stronger was the only law. The light of reason was not yet kindled, and the weak was entirely at the mercy of the strong. The weak individual then began to learn how to defend himself. He made use of a club, stone, spear, sling, or bow and arrow, and in the course of time, instead of physical strength, intelligence became the chief deciding factor in the battle. The wild character was gradually softened by the awakening of noble sentiments, and so, imperceptibly, after ages of continued progress, we have come from the brutal fight of the unreasoning animal to what we call the "civilized warfare" of to-day, in which the combatants shake hands, talk in a friendly way, and smoke cigars in the entr'actes, ready to engage again in deadly conflict at a signal. Let pessimists say what they like, here is an absolute evidence of great and gratifying advance.

But now, what is the next phase in this evolution? Not peace as yet, by any means. The next change which should naturally follow from modern developments should be the continuous diminution of the number of individuals engaged in battle. The apparatus will be one of specifically great power, but only a few individuals will be required to operate it. This evolution will bring more and more into prominence a machine or mechanism with the fewest individuals as an element of warfare, and the absolutely unavoidable consequence of this will be the abandonment of large, clumsy, slowly moving, and unmanageable units. Greatest possible speed and maximum rate of energy-delivery by the war apparatus will be the main object. The loss of life will become smaller and smaller, and finally, the number of the individuals continuously diminishing, merely machines will meet in a contest without blood-shed, the nations being simply interested, ambitious spectators. When this happy condition is realized, peace will be assured. But, no matter to what degree of perfection rapid-fire guns, high-power cannon, explosive projectiles, torpedo-boats, or other implements of war may be brought, no matter how destructive they may be made, that condition can never be reached through any such development. All such implements require men for their operation; men are indispensable parts of the machinery. Their object is to kill and to destroy. Their power resides in their capacity for doing evil. So long as men meet in battle, there will be bloodshed. Bloodshed will ever keep up barbarous passion. To break this fierce spirit, a radical departure must be made, an entirely new principle must be introduced, something that never existed before in warfare—a principle which will forcibly, unavoidably, turn the battle into a mere spectacle, a play, a contest without loss of blood. To bring on this result men must be dispensed with: machine must fight machine. But how accomplish that which seems impossible? The answer is simple enough: produce a machine capable of acting as though it were part of a human being—no mere mechanical contrivance, comprising levers, screws, wheels, clutches, and nothing more, but a machine embodying a higher principle, which will enable it to per form its duties as though it had intelligence, experience, judgment, a mind! This conclusion is the result of my thoughts and observations which have extended through virtually my whole life, and I shall now briefly describe how I came to accomplish that which at first seemed an unrealizable dream.

A long time ago, when I was a boy, I was afflicted with a singular trouble, which seems to have been due to an extraordinary excitability of the retina. It was the appearance of images which, by their persistence, marred the vision of real objects and interfered with thought. When a word was said to me, the image of the object which it designated would appear vividly before my eyes, and many times it was impossible for me to tell whether the object I saw was real or not. This caused me great discomfort and anxiety, and I tried hard to free myself of the spell. But for a long time I tried in vain, and it was not, as I clearly recollect, until I was about twelve years old that I succeeded for the first time, by an effort of the will, in banishing an image which presented itself. My happiness will never be as complete as it was then, but, unfortunately (as I thought at that time), the old trouble returned, and with it my anxiety. Here it was that the observations to which I refer began. I noted, namely, that whenever the image of an object appeared before my eyes I had seen something that reminded me of it. In the first instances I thought this to be purely accidental, but soon I convinced myself that it was not so. A visual impression, consciously or unconsciously received, invariably preceded the appearance of the image. Gradually the desire arose in me to find out, every time, what caused the images to appear, and the satisfaction of this desire soon became a necessity. The next observation I made was that, just as these images followed as a result of something I had seen, so also the thoughts which I conceived were suggested in like manner. Again, I experienced the same desire to locate the image which caused the thought, and this search for the original visual impression soon grew to be a second nature. Mt mind became automatic, as it were, and in the course of years of continued, almost unconscious performance, I acquired the ability of locating every time and, as a rule, instantly the visual impression which started the thought. Nor is this all. It was not long before I was aware that also all my movements were prompted in the same way, and so, searching, observing, and verifying continuously, year by year, I have, by every thought and every act of mine, demonstrated, and do so daily, to my absolute satisfaction, that I am an automaton endowed with power of movement, which merely responds to external stimuli beating upon my sense organs, and thinks and acts and moves accordingly. I remember only one or two cases in all my life in which I was unable to locate the first impression which prompted a movement or a thought, or even a dream.

With these experiences it was only natural that, long ago, I conceived the idea of constructing an automaton which would mechanically represent me, and which would respond, as I do myself, but, of course, in a much more primitive manner, to external influences. Such an automaton evidently had to have motive power, organs for locomotion, directive organs, and one or more sensitive organs so adapted as to be excited by external stimuli. This machine would, I reasoned, perform its movements in the manner of a living being, for it would have all the chief mechanical characteristics or elements of the same. There was still the capacity for growth, propagation, and, above all, the mind which would be wanting to make the model complete. But growth was not necessary in this case, since a machine could be manufactured full grown, so to speak. As to the capacity for propagation, it could likewise be left out of consideration, for in the mechanical model it merely signified a process of manufacture. Whether the automation be of flesh and bone, or of wood and steel, it mattered little, provided it could perform all the duties required of it like an intelligent being. To do so, it had to have an element corresponding to the mind, which would effect the control of all its movements and operations, and cause it to act, in any unforeseen case that might present itself, with knowledge, reason, judgment, and experience. But this element I could easily embody in it by conveying to it my own intelligence, my own understanding. So this invention was evolved, and so a new art came into existence, for which the name "telautomatics" has been suggested, which means the art of controlling the movements and operations of distant automatons.

FIG. 2. THE FIRST PRACTICAL TELAUTOMATON.

A machine having all the bodily or translatory movements and the operations of the interior mechanism controlled from a distance without wires. The crewless boat shown in the photograph contains its own motive power, propelling and steering machinery, and numerous other accessories, all of which are controlled by transmitting from a distance, without wires, electrical oscillations to a circuit carried by the boat and adjusted to respond only to these oscillations.

This principle evidently was applicable to any kind of machine that moves on land or in the water or in the air. In applying it practically for the first time, I selected a boat (see Fig. 2). A storage battery placed within it furnished the motive power. The propeller, driven by a motor, represented the locomotive organs. The rudder, controlled by another motor likewise driven by the battery, took the place of the directive organs. As to the sen-sitive organ, obviously the first thought was to utilize a device responsive to rays of light, like a selenium

FIG. 3. EXPERIMENT TO ILLUSTRATE THE SUPPLYING OF ELECTRICAL ENERGY THOUGH A SINGLE WIRE WITHOUT RETURN.

An ordinary incandescent lamp, connected with one or both of its terminals to the wire photograph, is lighted by electrical vibrations conveyed to it thorough the coil from an electrical oscillator, which is worked only to one fifth of on per cent of its capacity.

FIG. 4. EXPERIMENT TO ILLUSTRATE THE TRANSMISSION OF ELECTRICAL ENERGY THROUGH THE EARTH WITHOUT WIRE.

The coil shown in the photograph has its lower end or terminal connected to the ground, and is exactly attuned to the vibrations of a distant electrical oscillator. The lamp lighted is in an independent wire loop, energized by induction from the coil excited by the electrical vibrations transmitted to it through the ground from the oscillator, which is worked only to five per cent. of its full capacity.

cell, to represent the human eye. But upon closer inquiry I found that, owing to experimental and other difficulties, no thoroughly satisfactory control of the automaton could be effected by light, radiant heat, hertzian radiations, or by rays in general, that is, disturbances which pass in straight lines through space. One of the reasons was that any obstacle coming between the operator and the distant automaton would place it beyond his control. Another reason was that the sensitive device representing the eye would have to be in a definite position with respect to the distant controlling apparatus, and this necessity would impose great limitations in the control. Still another and very important reason was that, in using rays, it would be difficult, if not impossible, to give to the automaton individual features or characteristics distinguishing it from other machines of this kind. Evidently the automaton should respond only to an individual call, as a person responds to a name. Such considerations led me to conclude that the sensitive device of the machine should correspond to the ear rather than the eye of a human being, for in this case its actions could be controlled irrespective of intervening obstacles, regardless of its position relative to the distant controlling apparatus, and, last, but not least, it would remain deaf and unresponsive, like a faithful servant, to all calls but that of its master. These requirements made it imperative to use, in the control of the automaton, instead of light or other rays, waves or disturbances which propagate in all directions through space, like sound, or which follow a path of least resistance, however curved. I attained the result aimed at by means of an electric circuit placed within the boat, and adjusted, or "tuned," exactly to electrical vibrations of the proper kind transmitted to it from a distant "elec-

FIG. 5. PHOTOGRAPHIC VIEW OF THE COILS RESPONDING TO ELECTRICAL OSCILLATIONS.

The picture shows a number of coils , differently attuned and responding to the vibrations transmitted to them through the earth from an electrical oscillator. The large coil on the right, discharging strongly, is tuned to the fundamental vibration, which is fifty thousand per second; the two larger vertical coils to twice that number; the smaller white wire coil to four times that number, and the remaining small coils to higher tones. The vibrations produced by the oscillator were so intense that they affected perceptibly a small coil tuned to the twenty-sixth higher tone.

trical oscillator." This circuit, in responding, however feebly, to the transmitted vibrations, affected magnets and other contrivances, through the medium of which were controlled the movements of the propeller and rudder, and also the operations of numerous other appliances.

By the simple means described the knowledge, experience, judgment–the mind, so to speak–of the distant operator were embodied in that machine, which was thus enabled to move and to perform all its operations with reason and intelligence. It behaved just like a blindfolded person obeying directions received through the ear.

The automatons so far constructed had "borrowed minds," so to speak, as each merely formed part of the distant operator who conveyed to it his intelligent orders; but this art is only in the beginning. I purpose to show that, however impossible it may now seem, an automaton may be contrived which will have its "own mind," and by this I mean that it will be able, independent of any operator, left entirely to itself, to perform, in response to external influences affecting its sensitive organs, a great variety of acts and operations as if it had intelligence. It will be able to follow a course laid out or to obey orders given far in advance; it will be capable of distinguishing between what it ought and what it ought not to do, and of making experiences or, otherwise stated, of recording impressions which will definitely affect its subsequent actions. In fact, I have already conceived such a plan.

Although I evolved this invention many years ago and explained it to my visitors very frequently in my laboratory demonstrations, it was not until much later, long after I had perfected it, that it became known, when, naturally enough, it gave rise to much discussion and to sensational reports. But the true significance of this new art was not grasped by the majority, nor was the great force of the underlying principle recognized. As nearly as I could judge from the numerous comments which appeared, the results I had obtained were considered as entirely impossible. Even the few who were disposed to admit the practicability of the invention saw in it merely an automobile torpedo, which was to be used for the purpose of blowing up battleships, with doubtful success. The general impression was that I contemplated simply the steering of such a vessel by means of Hertzian or other rays. There are torpedoes steered electrically bywires, and there are means of communicating without wires, and the above was, of course an obvious inference. Had I accomplished nothing more than this, I should have made a small advance indeed. But the art I have evolved does not contemplate merely the change of direction of a

FIG. 6. PHOTOGRAPHIC VIEW OF THE ESSENTIAL PARTS OF THE ELECTRICAL OSCILLATOR USED IN THE EXPERIMENTS DESCRIBED

moving vessel; it affords means of absolutely controlling, in every respect, all the innumerable translatory movements, as well as the operations of all the internal organs, no matter how many, of an individualized automaton. Criticisms to the effect that the control of the automaton could be interfered with were made by people who do not even dream of the wonderful results which can be accomplished by use of electrical vibrations. The world moves slowly, and new truths are difficult to see. Certainly, by the use of this principle, an arm for attack as well as defense may be provided, of a destructiveness all the greater as the principle is applicable to submarine and aerial vessels. There is virtually no restriction as to the amount of explosive it can carry, or as to the distance at which it can strike, and failure is almost impossible. But the force of this new principle does not wholly reside in its destructiveness. Its advent introduces into warfare an element which never existed before–a fighting-machine without men as a means of attack and defense. The continuous development in this direction must ultimately make war a mere contest of machines without men and without loss of life–a condition which would have been impossible without this new departure, and which, in my opinion, must be reached as preliminary to permanent peace. The future will either bear out or disprove these views. My ideas on this subject have been put forth with deep conviction, but in a humble spirit.

The establishment of permanent peaceful relations between nations would most effectively reduce the force retarding the human mass, and would be the best solution of this great human problem. But will the dream of universal peace ever be realized? Let us hope that it will. When all darkness shall be dissipated by the light of science, when all nations shall be merged into one, and patriotism shall be identical with religion, when there shall be one language, one country, one end, then the dream will have become reality.

THE THIRD PROBLEM: HOW TO INCREASE THE FORCE ACCELERATING THE HUMAN MASS—THE HARNESSING OF THE SUN'S ENERGY.

Of the three possible solutions of the main problem of increasing human energy, this is by far the most important to consider, not only because of its intrinsic significance, but also because of its intimate bearing on all the many elements and conditions which determine the movement of humanity. In order to proceed systematically, it would be necessary for me to dwell on all those considerations which have guided me from the outset in my efforts to arrive at a solution, and which have led me, step by step, to the results I shall now describe. As a preliminary study of the problem an analytical investigation, such as I have made, of the chief forces which determine the onward movement, would be of advantage, particularly in conveying an idea of that hypothetical "velocity" which, as explained in the beginning, is a measure of human energy; but to deal with this specifically here, as I would desire, would lead me far beyond the scope of the present subject. Suffice it to state that the resultant of

FIG. 7. EXPERIMENT TO ILLUSTRATE AN INDUCTIVE EFFECT OF AN ELECTRICAL OSCILLATOR OF GREAT POWER.

The photograph shows three ordinary incandescent lamps lighted to full candle-power by currents induced in a local loop consisting of a single wire forming a square of fifty feet each side, which includes the lamps, and which is at a distance of one hundred feet from the primary circuit energized by the oscillator. The loop likewise includes an electrical condenser, and is exactly attuned to the vibrations of the oscillator, which is worked at less than five percent of its total capacity.

all these forces is always in the direction of reason, which therefore, determines, at any time, the direction of human movement. This is to say that every effort which is scientifically applied, rational, useful, or practical, must be in the direction in which the mass is moving. The practical, rational man, the observer, the man of business, he who reasons, calculates, or determines in advance, carefully applies his effort so that when coming into effect it will be in the direction of the movement, making it thus most efficient, and in this knowledge and ability lies the secret of his success. Every new fact discovered, every new experience or new element added to our knowledge and entering into the domain of reason, affects the same and, therefore, changes the direction of movement, which, however, must always take place along the resultant of all those efforts which, at that time, we designate as reasonable, that is, self-preserving, useful, profitable, or practical. These efforts concern our daily life, our necessities and comforts, our work and business, and it is these which drive man onward.

But looking at all this busy world about us, on all this complex mass as it daily throbs and moves, what is it but an immense clock-work driven by a

FIG. 8. EXPERIMENT TO ILLUSTRATE THE CAPACITY OF THE OSCILLATOR FOR PRODUCING ELECTRICAL EXPLOSIONS OF GREAT POWER.

Note to Fig. 8.–The coil, partly shown in the photograph, creates an alternative movement of electricity from the earth into a large reservoir and back at a rate of one hundred thousand alternations per second. The adjustments are such that the reservoir is filled full and bursts at each alternation just at the moment when the electrical pressure reaches the maximum. The discharge escapes with a deafening noise, striking an unconnected coil twenty-two feet away, and creating such a commotion of electricity in the earth that sparks an inch long can be drawn from a water main at a distance of three hundred feet from the laboratory.

spring? In the morning, when we rise, we cannot fail to note that all the objects about us are manufactured by machinery: the water we use is lifted by steam-power; the trains bring our breakfast from distant localities; the elevators in our dwelling and our office building, the cars that carry us there, are all driven by power; in all our daily errands, and in our very life-pursuit, we depend upon it; all the objects we see tell us of it; and when we return to our machine-made dwelling at night, lest we should forget it, all the material comforts of our home, our cheering stove and lamp, remind us of how much we depend on power. And when there is an accidental stoppage of the machinery, when the city is snowbound, or the life sustaining movement otherwise temporarily arrested, we are affrighted to realize how impossible it would be for us to live the life we live without motive power. Motive power means work. To increase the force accelerating human movement means, therefore, to perform more work.

So we find that the three possible solutions of the great problem of increasing human energy are answered by the three words: *food, peace, work.*

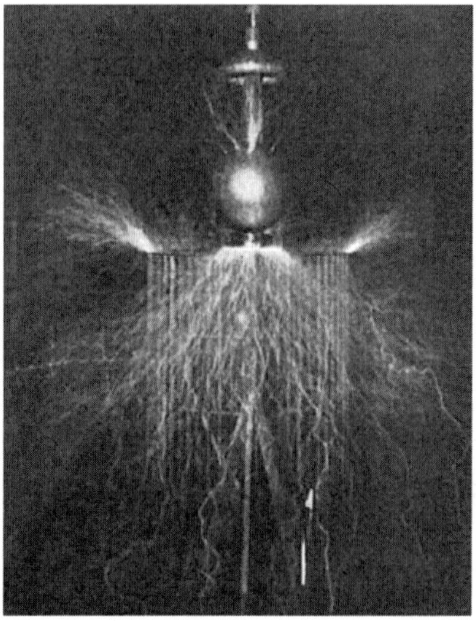

FIG. 9. EXPERIMENT TO ILLUSTRATE THE CAPACITY ON THE OSCILLATOR FOR CREATING A GREAT ELECTRICAL MOVEMENT.

The ball shown in the photograph, covered with a polished metallic coating of twenty square feet of surface, represents a large reservoir of electricity, and the inverted tin pan underneath, with a sharp rim, a big opening through which the electricity can escape before filling the reservoir. The quantity of electricity set in movement is so great that, although most of it escapes through the rim of the pan or opening provided, the ball or reservoir is nevertheless alternately emptied and filled to over-flowing (as is evident from the discharge escaping on the top of the ball) one hundred and fifty thousand times per second.

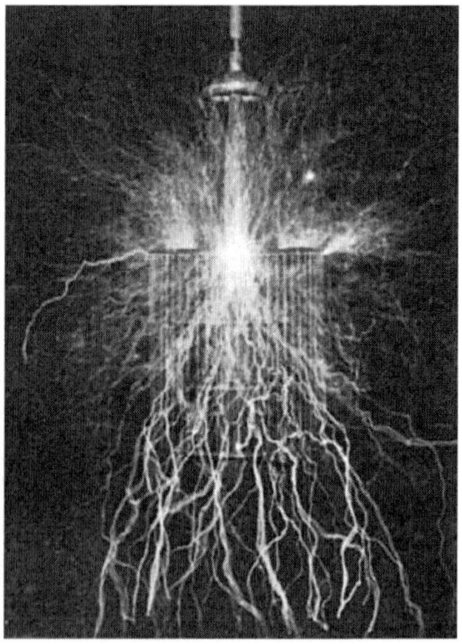

FIG. 10. PHOTOGRAPHIC VIEW OF AN EXPERIMENT TO ILLUSTRATE AN EFFECT OF AN ELECTRICAL OSCILLATOR DELIVERING ENERGY AT A RATE OF SEVENTY-FIVE THOUSAND HORSE-POWER.

The discharge, creating a strong draft owing to the heating of the air, is carried upward through the open roof of the building. The greatest width across is nearly seventy feet. The pressure is over twelve million volts, and the current alternates one hundred and thirty thousand times per second.

Many a year I have thought and pondered, lost myself in speculations and theories, considering man as a mass moved by a force, viewing his inexplicable movement in the light of a mechanical one, and applying the simple principles of mechanics to the analysis of the same until I arrived at these solutions, only to realize that they were taught to me in my early childhood. These three words sound the key-notes of the Christian religion. Their scientific meaning and purpose now clear to me: food to increase the mass, peace to diminish the retarding force, and work to increase the force accelerating human movement. These are the only three solutions which are possible of that great problem, and all of them have one object, one end, namely, to increase human energy. When we recognize this, we cannot help wondering how profoundly wise and scientific and how immensely practical the Christian religion is, and in what a marked contrast it stands in this respect to other religions. It is unmistakably the result of practical experiment and scientific observation which have extended through the ages, while other religions seem to be the outcome of merely abstract reasoning. Work, untiring effort, useful and accumulative, with periods of rest and recuperation aiming at higher efficiency, is its chief and ever-recurring command. Thus we are inspired both by Christianity and Science to do our utmost toward increasing the performance of mankind. This most important of human problems I shall now specifically consider.

THE SOURCE OF HUMAN ENERGY–THE THREE WAYS OF DRAWING ENERGY FROM THE SUN.

First let us ask: Whence comes all the motive power? What is the spring that drives all? We see the ocean rise and fall, the rivers flow, the wind, rain, hail, and snow beat on our windows, the trains and steamers come and go; we here the rattling noise of carriages, the voices from the street; we feel, smell, and taste; and we think of all this. And all this movement, from the surging of the mighty ocean to that subtle movement concerned in our thought, has but one common cause. All this energy emanates from one single center, one single source–the sun. The sun is the spring that drives all. The sun maintains all human life and supplies all human energy. Another answer we have now found to the above great question: To increase the force accelerating human movement means to turn to the uses of man more of the sun's energy. We honor and revere those great men of bygone times whose names are linked with immortal achievements, who have proved themselves benefactors of humanity–the religious reformer with his wise maxims of life, the philosopher with his deep truths, the mathematician with his formul–, the physicist with his laws, the discover with his principles and secrets wrested from nature, the artist with his forms of the beautiful; but who honors him, the greatest of all,–who can tell the name of him,–who first turned to use the sun's energy to save the effort of a weak fellow-creature? That was man's first act of scientific philanthropy, and its consequences have been incalculable.

From the very beginning three ways of drawing energy from the sun were open to man. The savage, when he warmed his frozen limbs at a fire kindled in some way, availed himself of the energy of the sun stored in the burning material. When he carried a bundle of branches to his cave and burned them there, he made use of the sun's stored energy transported from one to another locality. When he set sail to his canoe, he utilized the energy of the sun applied to the atmosphere or the ambient medium. There can be no doubt that the first is the oldest way. A fire, found accidentally, taught the savage to appreciate its beneficial heat. He then very likely conceived of the idea of carrying the glowing members to his abode. Finally he learned to use the force of a swift current of water or air. It is characteristic of modern development that progress has been effected in the same order. The utilization of the energy stored in wood or coal, or, generally speaking, fuel, led to the steam-engine. Next a great stride in advance was made in energy-transportation by the use of electricity, which permitted the transfer of energy from one locality to another without transporting the material. But as to the utilization of the energy of the ambient medium, no radical step forward has as yet been made known.

The ultimate results of development in these three directions are: first, the burning of coal by a cold process in a battery; second, the efficient utilization of the energy of the ambient medium; and, third the transmission without wires of electrical energy to any distance. In whatever way these results may be arrived at, their practical application will necessarily involve an extensive use of iron, and this invaluable metal will undoubtedly be an essential element in the further development along these three lines. If we succeed in burning coal by a cold process and thus obtain electrical energy in an efficient and inexpensive manner, we shall require in many practical uses of this energy electric motors–that is, iron. If we are successful in deriving energy from the ambient medium, we shall need, both in the obtainment and utilization of the energy, machinery–again, iron. If we realize the transmission of electrical energy without wires on an industrial scale, we shall be compelled to use extensively electric generators–once more, iron. Whatever we may do, iron will probably be the chief means of accomplishment in the near future, possibly more so than in the past. How long its reign will last is difficult to tell, for even now aluminium is looming up as a threatening competitor. But for the time being, next to providing new resources of energy, it is of the greatest importance to making improvements in the manufacture and utilization of iron. Great advances are possible in these latter directions, which, if brought about, would enormously increase the useful performance of mankind.

GREAT POSSIBILITIES OFFERED BY IRON FOR INCREASING HUMAN PERFORMANCE—ENORMOUS WASTE IN IRON MANUFACTURE.

Iron is by far the most important factor in modern progress. It contributes more than any other industrial product to the force accelerating human movement. So general is the use of this metal, and so intimately is it connected with all that concerns our life, that it has become as indispensable to us as the very air we breathe. Its name is synonymous with usefulness. But, however great the influence of iron may be on the present human development, it does not add to the force urging man onward nearly as much as it might. First of all, its manufacture as now carried on is connected with an appalling waste of fuel–that is, waste of energy. Then, again, only a part of all the iron produced is applied for useful purposes. A good part of it goes to create frictional resistances, while still another large part is the means of developing negative forces greatly retarding human movement. Thus the negative force of war is almost wholly represented in iron. It is impossible to estimate with any degree of accuracy the magnitude of this greatest of all retarding forces, but it is certainly very considerable. If the present positive impelling force due to all useful applications of iron be represented by ten, for instance, I should not think it exaggeration to estimate the negative force of war, with due consideration of all its retarding influences and results, at, say, six. On the basis of this estimate the effective impelling force of iron in the positive direction would be measured by the difference of these two numbers, which is four. But if, through the establishment of universal peace, the manufacture of war machinery should cease, and all struggle for supremacy between nations should be turned into healthful, ever active and productive commercial competition, then the positive impelling force due to iron would be measured by the sum of those two, numbers, which is sixteen–that is, this force would have four times its present value. This example is, of course, merely intended to give an idea of the immense increase in the useful performance of mankind which would result from a radical reform of the iron industries supplying the implements of warfare.

A similar inestimable advantage in the saving of energy available to man would be secured by obviating the great waste of coal which is inseparably connected with the present methods of manufacturing iron. In some countries, such as Great Britain, the hurtful effects of this squandering of fuel are beginning to be felt. The price of coal is constantly rising, and the poor are made to suffer more and more. Though we are still far from the dreaded "exhaustion of the coalfields," philanthropy commands us to invent novel methods of manufacturing iron, which will not involve such barbarous waste of this valuable material from which we derive at present most of our energy. It is our duty to coming generations to leave this store of energy intact for them, or at least not to touch it until we shall have perfected processes for burning coal more efficiently. Those who are coming after us will need fuel more than we do. We should be able to manufacture the iron we require by using the sun's energy, without wasting any coal at all. As an effort to this end the idea of smelting iron ores by electric currents obtained from the energy of falling water has naturally suggested itself to many. I have myself spent much time in endeavoring to evolve such a practical process, which would enable iron to be manufactured at small cost. After a prolonged investigation of the subject, finding that it was unprofitable to use the currents generated directly for smelting the ore, I devised a method which is far more economical.

ECONOMICAL PRODUCTION OF IRON BY A NEW PROCESS.

The industrial project, as I worked it out six years ago, contemplated the employment of the electric currents derived from the energy of a waterfall, not directly for smelting the ore, but for decomposing water for a preliminary step. To lessen the cost of the plant, I proposed to generate the currents in exceptionally cheap and simple dynamos, which I designed for this sole purpose. The hydrogen liberated in the electrolytic decomposition was to be burned or recombined with oxygen, not with that from which it was separated, but with that of the atmosphere. Thus very nearly the total electrical energy used up in the decomposition of the water would be recovered in the form of heat resulting from the recombination of the hydrogen. This heat was to be applied to the smelting of ore. The oxygen gained as a by-product of the decomposition of the water I intended to use for certain other industrial purposes, which would probably yield good financial returns, inasmuch as this is the cheapest way of obtaining this gas in large quantities. In any event, it could be employed to burn all kinds of refuse, cheap hydrocarbon, or coal of the most inferior quality which could not be burned in air or be otherwise utilized to advantage, and thus again a considerable amount of heat would be made available for the smelting of the ore. To increase the economy of the process I contemplated, furthermore, using an arrangement such that the hot metal and the products of combustion, coming out of the furnace, would give up their heat upon the cold ore going into the furnace, so that comparatively little of the heat energy would be lost in the smelting. I calculated that probably forty thousand pounds of iron could be produced per horse-power per annum by this method. Liberal allowances were made for those losses which are unavoidable, the above quantity being about half of that theoretically obtainable. Relying on this estimate and on practical data with reference to a certain kind of sand ore existing in abundance in the region of the Great Lakes, including cost of transportation and labor, I found that in some localities iron could be manufactured in this manner cheaper than by any of the adopted methods. This result would be obtained all the more surely if the oxygen obtained from the water, instead of being used for smelting of ore, as assumed, should be more profitably employed. Any new demand for this gas would secure a higher revenue from the plant, thus cheapening the iron. This project was advanced merely in the interest of industry. Some day, I hope, a beautiful industrial butterfly will come out of the dusty and shriveled chrysalis.

The production of iron from sand ores by a process of magnetic separation is highly commendable in principle, since it involves no waste of coal; but the usefulness of this method is largely reduced by the necessity of melting the iron afterward. As to the crushing of iron ore, I would consider it rational only if done by water-power, or by energy otherwise obtained without consumption of fuel. An electrolytic cold process, which would make it possible to extract iron cheaply, and also to mold it into the required forms without any fuel consumption, would, in my opinion, be a very great advance in iron manufacture. In common with some other metals, iron has so far resisted electrolytic treatment, but there can be no doubt that such a cold process will ultimately replace in metallurgy the present crude method of casting, and thus obviating the enormous waste of fuel necessitated by the repeated heating of metal in the foundries.

Up to a few decades ago the usefulness of iron was based almost wholly on its remarkable mechanical properties, but since the advent of the commercial dynamo and electric motor its value to mankind has been greatly increased by its unique magnetic qualities. As regards the latter, iron has been greatly improved of late. The signal progress began about thirteen years ago, when I discovered that in using soft Bessemer steel instead of wrought iron, as then customary, in an alternating motor, the performanceof the machine was doubled. I brought this fact to the attention of Mr. Albert Schmid, to whose untiring efforts and ability is largely due the supremacy of American electrical machinery, and who was then superintendent of an industrial corporation engaged in this field. Following my suggestion, he constructed transformers of steel, and they showed the same marked improvement. The investigation was then systematically continued under Mr. Schmid's guidance, the impurities being gradually eliminated from the"steel" (which was only such in name, for in reality it was pure soft iron), and soon a product resulted which admitted of little further improvement.

THE COMING OF AGE OF ALUMINIUM–DOOM OF THE COPPER INDUSTRY–THE GREAT CIVILIZING POTENCY OF THE NEW METAL.

With the advances made in iron of late years we have arrived virtually at the limits of improvement. We cannot hope to increase very materially its tensile strength, elasticity, hardness, or malleability, nor can we expect to make it much better as regards its magnetic qualities. More recently a notable gain was secured by the mixture of a small percentage of nickel with the iron, but there is not much room for further advance in this direction. New discoveries may be expected, but they cannot greatly add to the valuable properties of the metal, though they may considerably reduce the cost of manufacture. The immediate future of iron is assured by its cheapness and its unrivaled mechanical and magnetic qualities. These are such that no other product can compete with it now. But there can be no doubt that, at a time not very distant, iron, in many of its now uncontested domains, will have to pass the scepter to another: the coming age will be the age of aluminium. It is only seventy years since this wonderful metal was discovered by Woehler, and the aluminium industry, scarcely forty years old, commands already the attention of the entire world. Such rapid growth has not been recorded in the history of civilization before. Not long ago aluminium was sold at the fanciful price of thirty or forty dollars per pound; to-day it can be had in any desired amount for as many cents. What is more, the time is not far off when this price, too, will be considered fanciful, for great improvements are possible in the methods of its manufacture. Most of the metal is now produced in the electric furnace by a process combining fusion and electrolysis, which offers a number of advantageous features, but involves naturally a great waste of the electrical energy of the current. My estimates show that the price of aluminium could be considerably reduced by adopting in its manufacture a method similar to that proposed by me for the production of iron. A pound of aluminium requires for fusion only about seventy per cent. of the heat needed for melting a pound of iron, and inasmuch as its weight is only about one third of that of the latter, a volume of aluminium four times that of iron could be obtained from a given amount of heat-energy. But a cold electrolytic process of manufacture is the ideal solution, and on this I have placed my hope.

The absolutely unavoidable consequence of the advancement of the aluminium industry will be the annihilation of the copper industry. They cannot exist and prosper together, and the latter is doomed beyond any hope of recovery. Even now it is cheaper to convey an electric current through aluminium wires than through copper wires; aluminium castings cost less, and in many domestic and other uses copper has no chance of successfully competing. A further material reduction of the price of aluminium cannot but be fatal to copper. But the progress of the former will not go on unchecked, for, as it ever happens in such cases, the larger industry will absorb the smaller one: the giant copper interests willcontrol the pygmy aluminium interests, and the slow-pacing copper will reduce the lively gait of aluminium. This will only delay, not avoid the impending catastrophe.

Aluminium, however, will not stop at downing copper. Before many years have passed it will be engaged in a fierce struggle with iron, and in the latter it will find an adversary not easy to conquer. The issue of the contest will largely depend on whether iron shall be indispensable in electric machinery. This the future alone can decide. Themagnetism as exhibited in iron is an isolated phenomenon in nature. What it is that makes this metal behave so radically different from all other materials in this respect has not yet been ascertained, though many theories have been suggested. As regards magnetism, the molecules of the various bodies behave like hollow beams partly filled with a heavy fluid and balanced in the middle in the manner of a see-saw. Evidently some disturbing influence exists in nature which causes each molecule, like such a beam, to tilt either one or the other way. If the molecules are tilted one way, the body is magnetic; if they are tilted the other way, the body is non-magnetic; but both positions are stable, as they would be in the case of the hollow beam, owing to the rush of the fluid to the lower end. Now, the wonderful thing is that the molecules of all known bodies went one way, while those of iron went the other way. This metal, it would seem, has an origin entirely different from that of the rest of the globe. It is highly improbable that we shall discover some other and cheaper material which will equal or surpass iron in magnetic qualities.

Unless we should make a radical departure in the character of the electric currents employed, iron will be indispensable. Yet the advantages it offers are only apparent. So long as we use feeble magnetic forces it is by far superior to any other material; but if we find ways of producing great magnetic forces, than better results will be obtainable without it. In fact, I have already produced electric transformers in which no iron is employed, and which are capable of performing ten times as much work per pound of weight as those of iron. This result is attained by using electric currents of a very high rate of vibration, produced in novel ways, instead of the ordinary currents now employed in the industries. I have also succeeded in operating electric motors without iron by such rapidly vibrating currents, but the results, so far, have been inferior to those obtained with ordinary motors constructed of iron, although theoretically the former should be capable of performing incomparably more work per unit of weight than the latter. But the seemingly insuperable difficulties which are now in the way may be overcome in the end, and then iron will be done away with, and all electric machinery will be manufactured of aluminium, in all probability, at prices ridiculously low. This would be a severe, if not fatal, blow to iron. In many other branches of industry, as ship-building, or wherever lightness of structure is required, the progress of the new metal will be much quicker. For such uses it is eminently suitable, and is sure to supersede iron sooner or later. It is highly probable that in the course of time we shall be able to give it many of those qualities which make iron so valuable.

While it is impossible to tell when this industrial revolution will be consummated, there can be no doubt that the future belongs to aluminium, and that in times to come it will be the chief means of increasing human performance. It has in this respect capacities greater by far than those of any other metal. I should estimate its civilizing potency at fully one hundred times that of iron. This estimate, though it may astonish, is not at all exaggerated. First of all, we must remember that there is thirty times as much aluminium as iron in bulk, available for the uses of man. This in itself offers great possibilities. Then, again, the new metal is much more easily workable, which adds to its value. In many of its properties it partakes of the character of a precious metal, which gives it additional worth. Its electric conductivity, which, for a given weight, is greater than that of any other metal, would be alone sufficient to make it one of the most important factors in future human progress. Its extreme lightness makes it far more easy to transport the objects manufactured. By virtue of this property it will revolutionize naval construction, and in facilitating transport and travel it will add enormously to the useful performance of mankind. But its greatest civilizing property will be, I believe, in a–rial travel, which is sure to be brought about by means of it. Telegraphic instruments will slowly enlighten the barbarian. Electric motors and lamps will do it more quickly, but quicker than anything else the flying-machine will do it. By rendering travel ideally easy it will be the best means for unifying the heterogeneous elements of humanity. As the first step toward this realization we should produce a lighter storage-battery or get more energy from coal.

EFFORTS TOWARD OBTAINING MORE ENERGY FROM COAL–THE ELECTRIC TRANSMISSION–THE GAS-ENGINE–THE COLD-COAL BATTERY.

I remember that at one time I considered the production of electricity by burning coal in a battery as the greatest achievement toward the advancing civilization, and I am surprised to find how much the continuous study of these subjects has modified my views. It now seems to me that to burn coal, however efficiently, in a battery would be a mere makeshift, a phase in the evolution toward something much more perfect. After all, in generating electricity in this manner, we should be destroying material, and this would be a barbarous process. We ought to be able to obtain the energy we need without consumption of material. But I am far from underrating the value of such an efficient method of burning fuel. At the present time most motive power comes from coal, and, either directly or by its products, it adds vastly to human energy. Unfortunately, in all the process now adopted, the larger portion of the energy of the coal is uselessly dissipated. The best steam-engines utilize only a small part of the total energy. Even in gas-engines, in which, particularly of late, better results are obtainable, there is still a barbarous waste going on. In our electric-lighting systems we scarcely utilize one third of one per cent., and in lighting by gas a much smaller fraction, of the total energy of the coal. Considering the various uses of coal throughout the world, we certainly do not utilize more than two per cent. of its energy theoretically available. The man who should stop this senseless waste would be a great benefactor of humanity, though the solution he would offer could not be a permanent one, since it would ultimately lead to the exhaustion of the store of material. Efforts toward obtaining more energy from coal are now being made chiefly in two directions–by generating electricity and by producing gas for motive-power purposes. In both of these lines notable success has already been achieved.

The advent of the alternating-current system of electric power-transmission marks an epoch in the economy of energy available to man from coal. Evidently all electrical energy obtained from a waterfall, saving so much fuel, is a net gain to mankind, which is all the more effective as it is secured with little expenditure of human effort, and as this most perfect of all known methods of deriving energy from the sun contributes in many ways to the advancement of civilization. But electricity enables us also to get from coal much more energy than was practicable in the old ways. Instead of transporting the coal to distant places of consumption, we burn it near the mine, develop electricity in the dynamos, and transmit the current to remote localities, thus effecting a considerable saving. Instead of driving the machinery in a factory in the old wasteful way of belts and shafting, we generate electricity by steam-power and operate electric motors. In this manner it is not uncommon to obtain two or three times as much effective motive power from the fuel, besides securing many other important advantages. It is in this field as much as in the transmission of energy to great distance that the alternating system, with its ideally simple machinery, is bringing about an industrial revolution. But in many lines this progress has not been yet fully felt. For example, steamers and trains are still being propelled by the direct application of steam-power to shafts or axles. A much greater percentage of the heat-energy of the fuel could be transformed into motive energy by using, in place of the adopted marine engines and locomotives, dynamos driven by specially designed high-pressure steam- or gas-engines and by utilizing the electricity generated for the propulsion. A gain of fifty to one hundred per cent. in the effective energy derived from the coal could be secured in this manner. It is difficulty to understand why a fact so plain and obvious is not receiving more attention from engineers. In ocean steamers such an improvement would be particularly desirable, as it would do away with noise and increase materially the speed and the carrying capacity of the liners.

Still more energy is now being obtained from coal by the latest improved gas-engine, the economy of which is, on the average, probably twice that of the best steam-engine. The introduction of the gas-engine is very much facilitated by the importance of the gas industry. With the increasing use of the electric light more and more of the gas is utilized for heating and motive-power purposes. In many instances gas is manufactured close to the coal-mine and conveyed to distant places of consumption, a considerable saving both in cost of transportation and in utilization of the energy of the fuel being thus effected. In the present state of the mechanical and electrical arts the most rational way of deriving energy from coal is evidently to manufacture gas close to the coal store, and to utilize it, either on the spot or elsewhere, to generate electricity for industrial uses in dynamos driven by gas engines. The commercial success of such a plant is largely dependent upon the production of gas-engines of great nominal horse-power, which, judging from the keen activity in this field will soon be forthcoming. Instead of consuming coal directly, as usual, gas should be manufactured from it and burned to economize energy.

But all such improvements cannot be more than passing phases in the evolution toward something far more perfect, for ultimately we must succeed in obtaining electricity from coal in a more direct way, involving no great loss of heat-energy. Whether coal can be oxidized by a cold process is still a question. Its combination with oxygen always involves heat, and whether the energy of the combination of the carbon with another element can be turned directly into electrical energy has not yet been determined. Under certain conditions nitric acid will burn the carbon, generating an electric current, but the solution does not remain cold. Other means of oxidizing coal have been proposed, but they have offered no promise of leading to an efficient process. My own lack of success has been complete, though perhaps not quite so complete as that of some who have "perfected" the cold-coal battery. This problem is essentially one for the chemist to solve. It is not for the physicist, who determines all his results in advance, so that, when the experiment is tried, it cannot fail. Chemistry, though a positive science, does not yet admit of a solution by such positive methods as those which are available in the treatment of many physical problems. The result, if possible, will be arrived at through patent trying rather than through deduction or calculation. The time will soon come, however, when the chemist will be able to follow a course clearly mapped out beforehand, and when the process of his arriving at a desired result will be purely constructive. The cold-coal battery would give a great impetus to electrical development; it would lead very shortly to a practical flying-machine, and would enormously enhance the introduction of the automobile. But these and many other problems will be better solved, and in a more scientific manner, by a light storage battery.

ENERGY FROM THE MEDIUM–THE WINDMILL AND THE SOLAR ENGINE,–MOTIVE POWER FROM TERRESTRIAL HEAT–ELECTRICITY FROM NATURAL SOURCES.

Besides fuel, there is abundant material from which we might eventually derive power. An immense amount of energy is locked up in limestone, for instance, and machines can be driven by liberating the carbonic acid through sulphuric acid or otherwise. I once constructed such an engine, and it operated satisfactorily.

But, whatever our resources of primary energy may be in the future, we must, to be rational, obtain it without consumption of any material. Long ago I came to this conclusion, and to arrive at this result only two ways, as before indicated, appeared possible–either to turn to use the energy of the sun stored in the ambient medium, or to transmit, through the medium, the sun's energy to distant places from some locality where it was obtainable without consumption of material. At that time I at once rejected the latter method as entirely impracticable, and turned to examine the possibilities of the former.

It is difficult to believe, but it is, nevertheless, a fact, that since time immemorial man has had at his disposal a fairly good machine which has enabled him to utilize the energy of the ambient medium. This machine is the windmill. Contrary to popular belief, the power obtainable from wind is very considerable. Many a deluded inventor has spent years of his life in endeavoring to "harness the tides," and some have even proposed to compress air by tide- or wave-power for supplying energy, never understanding the signs of the old windmill on the hill, as it sorrowfully waved its arms about and bade them stop. The fact is that a wave- or tide-motor would have, as a rule, but a small chance of competing commercially with the windmill, which is by far the better machine, allowing a much greater amount of energy to be obtained in a simpler way. Wind-power has been, in old times, of inestimable value to man, if for nothing else but for enabling him, to cross the seas, and it is even now a very important factor in travel and transportation. But there are great limitations in this ideally simple method of utilizing the sun's energy. The machines are large for a given output, and the power is intermittent, thus necessitating the storage of energy and increasing the cost of the plant.

A far better way, however, to obtain power would be to avail ourselves of the sun's rays, which beat the earth incessantly and supply energy at a maximum rate of over four million horsepower per square mile. Although the average energy received per square mile in any locality during the year is only a small fraction of that amount, yet an inexhaustible source of power would be opened up by the discovery of some efficient method of utilizing the energy of the rays. The only rational way known to me at the time when I began the study of this subject was to employ some kind of heat- or thermodynamic-engine, driven by a volatile fluid evaporate in a boiler by the heat of the rays. But closer investigation of this method, and calculation, showed that, notwithstanding the apparently vast amount of energy received from the sun's rays, only a small fraction of that energy could be actually utilized in this manner. Furthermore, the energy supplied through the sun's radiations is periodical, and the same limitations as in the use of the windmill I found to exist here also. After a long study of this mode of obtaining motive power from the sun, taking into account the necessarily large bulk of the boiler, the low efficiency of the heat-engine, the additional cost of storing the energy and other drawbacks, I came to the conclusion that the "solar engine," a few instances excepted, could not be industrially exploited with success.

Another way of getting motive power from the medium without consuming any material would be to utilize the heat contained in the earth, the water, or the air for driving an engine. It is a well-known fact that the interior portions of the globe are very hot, the temperature rising, as observations show, with the approach to the center at the rate of approximately 1 degree C. for every hundred feet of depth. The difficulties of sinking shafts and placing boilers at depths of, say, twelve thousand feet, corresponding to an increase in temperature of about 120 degrees C., are not insuperable, and we could certainly avail ourselves in this way of the internal heat of the globe. In fact, it would not be necessary to go to any depth at all in order to derive energy from the stored terrestrial heat. The superficial layers of the earth and the air strata close to the same are at a temperature sufficiently high to evaporate some extremely volatile substances, which we might use in our boilers instead of water. There is no doubt that a vessel might be propelled on the ocean by an engine driven by such a volatile fluid, no other energy being used but the heat abstracted from the water. But the amount of power which could be obtained in this manner would be, without further provision, very small.

Electricity produced by natural causes is another source of energy which might be rendered available. Lightning discharges involve great amounts of electrical energy, which we could utilize by transforming and storing it. Some years ago I made known a method of electrical transformation which renders the first part of this task easy, but the storing of the energy of lightning discharges will be difficult to accomplish. It is well known, furthermore, that electric currents circulate constantly through the earth, and that there exists between the earth and any air stratum a difference of electrical pressure, which varies in proportion to the height.

In recent experiments I have discovered two novel facts of importance in this connection. One of these facts is that an electric current is generated in a wire extending from the ground to a great height by the axial, and probably also by the translatory, movement of the earth. No appreciable current, however, will flow continuously in the wire unless the electricity is allowed to leak out into the air. Its escape is greatly facilitated by providing at the elevated end of the wire a conducting terminal of great surface, with many sharp edges or points. We are thus enabled to get a continuous supply of electrical energy by merely supporting a wire at a height, but, unfortunately, the amount of electricity which can be so obtained is small.

The second fact which I have ascertained is that the upper air strata are permanently charged with electricity opposite to that of the earth. So, at least, I have interpreted my observations, from which it appears that the earth, with its adjacent insulating and outer conducting envelope, constitutes a highly charged electrical condenser containing, in all probability, a great amount of electrical energy which might be turned to the uses of man, if it were possible to reach with a wire to great altitudes.

It is possible, and even probable, that there will be, in time, other resources of energy opened up, of which we have no knowledge now. We may even find ways of applying forces such as magnetism or gravity for driving machinery without using any other means. Such realizations, though highly improbable, are not impossible. An example will best convey an idea of what we can hope to attain and what we can never attain. Imagine a disk of some homogeneous material turned perfectly true and arranged to turn in frictionless bearings on a horizontal shaft above the ground. This disk, being under the above conditions perfectly balanced, would rest in any position. Now, it is possible that we may learn how to make such a disk rotate continuously and perform work by the force of gravity without any further effort on our part; but it is perfectly impossible for the disk to turn and to do work without any force from the outside. If it could do so, it would be what is designated scientifically as a "perpetuum mobile," a machine creating its own motive power. To make the disk rotate by the force of gravity we have only to invent a screen against this force. By such a screen we could prevent this force from acting on one half of the disk, and the rotation of the latter would follow. At least, we cannot deny such a possibility until we know exactly the nature of the force of gravity. Suppose that this force were due to a movement comparable to that of a stream of air passing from above toward the center of the earth. The effect of such a stream upon both halves of the disk would be equal, and the latter would not rotate ordinarily; but if one half should be guarded by a plate arresting the movement, then it would turn.

A DEPARTURE FROM KNOWN METHODS–POSSIBILITY OF A "SELF-ACTING" ENGINE OR MACHINE, INANIMATE, YET CAPABLE, LIKE A LIVING BEING, OF DERIVING ENERGY FROM THE MEDIUM–THE IDEAL WAY OF OBTAINING MOTIVE POWER.

When I began the investigation of the subject under consideration, and when the preceding or similar ideas presented themselves to me for the first time, though I was then unacquainted with a number of the facts mentioned, a survey of the various ways of utilizing the energy of the medium convinced me, nevertheless, that to arrive at a thoroughly satisfactory practical solution a radical departure from the methods then known had to be made. The windmill, the solar engine, the engine driven by terrestrial heat, had their limitations in the amount of power obtainable. Some new way had to be discovered which would enable us to get more energy. There was enough heat-energy in the medium, but only a small part of it was available for the operation of an engine in the ways then known. Besides, the energy was obtainable only at a very slow rate. Clearly, then, the problem was to discover some new method which would make it possible both to utilize more of the heat-energy of the medium and also to draw it away from the same at a more rapid rate.

I was vainly endeavoring to form an idea of how this might be accomplished, when I read some statements from Carnot and Lord Kelvin (then Sir William Thomson) which meant virtually that it is impossible for an inanimate mechanism or self-acting machine to cool a portion of the medium below the temperature of the surrounding, and operate by the heat abstracted. These statements interested me intensely. Evidently a living being could do this very thing, and since the experiences of my early life which I have related had convinced me that a living being is only an automaton, or, otherwise stated, a "self-acting-engine," I came to the conclusion that it was possible to construct a machine which would do the same. As the first step toward this realization I conceived the following mechanism. Imagine a thermopile consisting of a number of bars of metal extending from the earth to the outer space beyond the atmosphere. The heat from below, conducted upward along these metal bars, would cool the earth or the sea or the air, according to the location of the lower parts of the bars, and the result, as is well known, would be an electric current circulating in these bars. The two terminals of the thermopile could now be joined through an electric motor, and, theoretically, this motor would run on and on, until the media below would be cooled down to the temperature of the outer space. This would be an inanimate engine which, to all evidence, would be cooling a portion of the medium below the temperature of the surrounding, and operating by the heat abstracted.

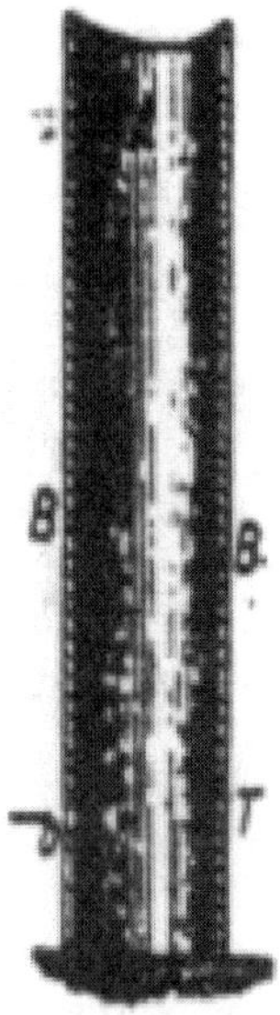

DIAGRAM* b. *OBTAINING ENERGY FROM THE AMBIENT MEDIUM

A, medium with little energy; *B*, *B*, ambient medium with much energy; *O*, path of the energy.

But was it not possible to realize a similar condition without necessarily going to a height? Conceive, for the sake of illustration, [a cylindrical] enclosure T, as illustrated in diagram b, such that energy could not be transferred across it except through a channel or path O, and that, by some means or other, in this enclosure a medium weremaintained which would have little energy, and that on the outer side of the same there would be the ordinary ambient medium with much energy. Under these assumptions the energy would flow through the path O, as indicated by the arrow, and might then be converted on its passage into some other form of energy. The question was, Could such a condition be attained? Could we produce artificially such a "sink" for the energy of the ambient medium to flow in? Suppose that an extremely low temperature could be maintained by some process in a given space; the surrounding medium would then be compelled to give off heat, which could be converted into mechanical or other form of energy, and utilized. By realizing such a plan, we should be enabled to get at any point of the globe a continuous supply of energy, day and night. More than this, reasoning in the abstract, it would seem possible to cause a quick circulation of the medium, and thus draw the energy at a very rapid rate.

Here, then, was an idea which, if realizable, afforded a happy solution of the problem of getting energy from the medium. But was it realizable? I convinced myself that it was so in a number of ways, of which one is the following. As regards heat, we are at a high level, which may be represented by the surface of a mountain lake considerably above the sea, the level of which may mark the absolute zero of temperature existing in the interstellar space. Heat, like water, flows from high to low level, and, consequently, just as we can let the water of the lake run down to the sea, so we are able to let heat from the earth's surface travel up into the cold region above. Heat, like water, can perform work in flowing down, and if we had any doubt as to whether we could derive energy from the medium by means of a thermopile, as before described, it would be dispelled by this analogue. But can we produce cold in a given portion of the space and cause the heat to flow in continually? To create such a "sink," or "cold hole," as we might say, in the medium, would be equivalent to producing in the lake a space either empty or filled with something much lighter than water. This we could do by placing in the lake a tank, and pumping all the water out of the latter. We know, then, that the water, if allowed to flow back into the tank, would, theoretically, be able to perform exactly the same amount of work which was used in pumping it out, but not a bit more. Consequently nothing could be gained in this double operation of first raising the water and then letting it fall down. This would mean that it is impossible to create such a sink in the medium. But let us reflect a moment. Heat, though following certain general laws of mechanics, like a fluid, is not such; it is energy which may be converted into other forms of energy as it passes from a high to a low level. To make our mechanical analogy complete and true, we must, therefore, assume that the water, in its passage into the tank, is converted into something else, which may be taken out of it without using any, or by using very little, power. For example, if heat be represented in this analogue by the water of the lake, the oxygen and hydrogen composing the water may illustrate other forms of energy into which the heat is transformed in passing from hot to cold. If the process of heat transformation were absolutely perfect, no heat at all would arrive at the low level, since all of it would be converted into other forms of energy. Corresponding to this ideal case, all the water flowing into the tank would be decomposed into oxygen and hydrogen before reaching the bottom, and the result would be that water would continually flow in, and yet the tank would remain entirely empty, the gases formed escaping. We would thus produce, by expending initially a certain amount of work to create a sink for the heat or, respectively, the water to flow in, a condition enabling us to get any amount of energy without further effort. This would be an ideal way of obtaining motive power. We do not know of any such absolutely perfect process of heat-conversion, and consequently some heat will generally reach the low level, which means to say, in our mechanical analogue, that some water will arrive at the bottom of the tank, and a gradual and slow filling of the latter will take place, necessitating continuous pumping out. But evidently there will be less to pump out than flows in, or, in other words, less energy will be needed to maintain the initial condition than is developed by the fall, and this is to say that some energy will be gained from the medium. What is not converted in flowing down can just be raised up with its own energy, and what is converted is clear gain. Thus the virtue of the principle I have discovered resides wholly in the conversion of the energy on the downward flow.

FIRST EFFORTS TO PRODUCE THE SELF-ACTING ENGINE–THE MECHANICAL OSCILLATOR–WORK OF DEWAR AND LINDE–LIQUID AIR.

Having recognized this truth, I began to devise means for carrying out my idea, and, after long thought, I finally conceived a combination of apparatus which should make possible the obtaining of power from the medium by a process of continuous cooling of atmospheric air. This apparatus, by continually transforming heat into mechanical work, tended to become colder and colder, and if it only were practicable to reach a very low temperature in this manner, then a sink for the heat could be produced, and energy could be derived from the medium. This seemed to be contrary to the statements of Carnot and Lord Kelvin before referred to, but I concluded from the theory of the process that such a result could be attained. This conclusion I reached, I think, in the latter part of 1883, when I was in Paris, and it was at a time when my mind was being more and more dominated by an invention which I had evolved during the preceding year, and which has since become known under the name of the "rotating magnetic field." During the few years which followed I elaborated further the plan I had imagined, and studied the working conditions, but made little headway. The commercial introduction in this country of the invention before referred to required most of my energies until 1889, when I again took up the idea of the self-acting machine. A closer investigation of the principles involved, and calculation, now showed that the result I aimed at could not be reached in a practical manner by ordinary machinery, as I had in the beginning expected. This led me, as a next step, to the study of a type of engine generally designated as "turbine," which at first seemed to offer better chances for a realization of the idea. Soon I found, however, that the turbine, too, was unsuitable. But my conclusions showed that if an engine of a peculiar kind could be brought to a high degree of perfection, the plan I had conceived was realizable, and I resolved to proceed with the development of such an engine, the primary object of which was to secure the greatest economy of transformation of heat into mechanical energy. A characteristic feature of the engine was that the work-performing piston was not connected with anything else, but was perfectly free to vibrate at an enormous rate. The mechanical difficulties encountered in the construction of this engine were greater than I had anticipated, and I made slow progress. This work was continued until early in 1892, when I went to London, where I saw Professor Dewar's admirable experiments with liquefied gases. Others had liquefied gases before, and notably Ozlewski and Pictet had performed creditable early experiments in this line, but there was such a vigor about the work of Dewar that even the old appeared new. His experiments showed, though in a way different from that I had imagined, that it was possible to reach a very low temperature by transforming heat into mechanical work, and I returned, deeply impressed with what I had seen, and more than ever convinced that my plan was practicable. The work temporarily interrupted was taken up anew, and soon I had in a fair state of perfection the engine which I have named "the mechanical oscillator." In this machine I succeeded in doing away with all packings, valves, and lubrication, and in producing so rapid a vibration of the piston that shafts of tough steel, fastened to the same and vibrated longitudinally, were torn asunder. By combining this engine with a dynamo of special design I produced a highly efficient electrical generator, invaluable in measurements and determinations of physical quantities on account of the unvarying rate of oscillation obtainable by its means. I exhibited several types of this machine, named "mechanical and electrical oscillator," before the Electrical Congress at the World's Fair in Chicago during the summer of 1893, in a lecture which, on account of other pressing work, I was unable to prepare for publication. On that occasion I exposed the principles of the mechanical oscillator, but the original purpose of this machine is explained here for the first time.

In the process, as I had primarily conceived it, for the utilization of the energy of the ambient medium, there were five essential elements in combination, and each of these had to be newly designed and perfected, as no such machines existed. The mechanical oscillator was the first element of this combination, and having perfected this, I turned to the next, which was an air-compressor of a design in certain respects resembling that of the mechanical oscillator. Similar difficulties in the construction were again encountered, but the work was pushed vigorously, and at the close of 1894 I had completed these two elements of the combination, and thus produced an apparatus for compressing air, virtually to any desired pressure, incomparably simpler, smaller, and more efficient than the ordinary. I was just beginning work on the third element, which together with the first two would give a refrigerating machine of exceptional efficiency and simplicity, when a misfortune befell me in the burning of my laboratory, which crippled my labors and delayed me. Shortly afterward Dr. Carl Linde announced the liquefaction of air by a self-cooling process, demonstrating that it was practicable to proceed with the cooling until liquefaction of the air took place. This was the only experimental proof which I was still wanting that energy was obtainable from the medium in the manner contemplated by me.

The liquefaction of air by a self-cooling process was not, as popularly believed, an accidental discovery, but a scientific result which could not have been delayed much longer, and which, in all probability, could not have escaped Dewar. This fascinating advance, I believe, is largely due to the powerful work of this great Scotchman. Nevertheless, Linde's is an immortal achievement. The manufacture of liquid air has been carried on for four years in Germany, on a scale much larger than in any other country, and this strange product has been applied for a variety of purposes. Much was expected of it in the beginning, but so far it has been an industrial ignis fatuus. By the use of such machinery as I am perfecting, its cost will probably be greatly lessened, but even then its commercial success will be questionable. When, used as a refrigerant it is uneconomical, as its temperature is unnecessarily low. It is as expensive to maintain a body at a very low temperature as it is to keep it very hot; it takes coal to keep air cold. In oxygen manufacture it cannot yet compete with the electrolytic method. For use as an explosive it is unsuitable, because its low temperature again condemns it to a small efficiency, and for motive-power purposes its cost is still by far too high. It is of interest to note, however, that in driving an engine by liquid air a certain amount of energy may be gained from the engine, or, stated otherwise, from the ambient medium which keeps the engine warm, each two hundred pounds of iron-casting of the latter contributing energy at the rate of about one effective horsepower during one hour. But this gain of the consumer is offset by an equal loss of the producer.

Much of this task on which I have labored so long remains to be done. A number of mechanical details are still to be perfected and some difficulties of a different nature to be mastered, and I cannot hope to produce a self-acting machine deriving energy from the ambient medium for a long time yet, even if all my expectations should materialize. Many circumstances have occurred which have retarded my work of late, but for several reasons the delay was beneficial.

One of these reasons was that I had ample time to consider what the ultimate possibilities of this development might be. I worked for a long time fully convinced that the practical realization of this method of obtaining energy from the sun would be of incalculable industrial value, but the continued study of the subject revealed the fact that while it will be commercially profitable if my expectations are well founded, it will not be so to an extraordinary degree.

DISCOVERY OF UNEXPECTED PROPERTIES OF THE ATMOSPHERE–STRANGE EXPERIMENTS–TRANSMISSION OF ELECTRICAL ENERGY THROUGH ONE WIRE WITHOUT RETURN–TRANSMISSION THROUGH THE EARTH WITHOUT ANY WIRE.

Another of these reasons was that I was led to recognize the transmission of electrical energy to any distance through the media as by far the best solution of the great problem of harnessing the sun's energy for the uses of man. For a long time I was convinced that such a transmission on an industrial scale, could never be realized, but a discovery which I made changed my view. I observed that under certain conditions the atmosphere, which is normally a high insulator, assumes conducting properties, and so becomes capable of conveying any amount of electrical energy. But the difficulties in the way of a practical utilization of this discovery for the purpose of transmitting electrical energy without wires were seemingly insuperable. Electrical pressures of many millions of volts had to be produced and handled; generating apparatus of a novel kind, capable of withstanding the immense electrical stresses, had to be invented and perfected, and a complete safety against the dangers of the high-tension currents had to be attained in the system before its practical introduction could be even thought of. All this could not be done in a few weeks or months, or even years. The work required patience and constant application, but the improvements came, though slowly. Other valuable results were, however, arrived at in the course of this long-continued work, of which I shall endeavor to give a brief account, enumerating the chief advances as they were successively effected.

The discovery of the conducting properties of the air, though unexpected, was only a natural result of experiments in a special field which I had carried on for some years before. It was, I believe, during 1889 that certain possibilities offered by extremely rapid electrical oscillations determined me to design a number of special machines adapted for their investigation. Owing to the peculiar requirements, the construction of these machines was very difficult, and consumed much time and effort; but my work on them was generously rewarded, for I reached by their means several novel and important results. One of the earliest observations I made with these new machines was that electrical oscillations of an extremely high rate act in an extraordinary manner upon the human organism. Thus, for instance, I demonstrated that powerful electrical discharges of several hundred thousand volts, which at that time were considered absolutely deadly, could be passed through the body without inconvenience or hurtful consequences. These oscillations produced other specific physiological effects, which, upon my announcement, were eagerly taken up by skilled physicians and further investigated. This new field has proved itself fruitful beyond expectation, and in the few years which have passed since, it has been developed to such an extent that it now forms a legitimate and important department of medical science. Many results, thought impossible at that time, are now readily obtainable with these oscillations, and many experiments undreamed of then can now be readily performed by their means. I still remember with pleasure how, nine years ago, I passed the discharge of a powerful induction-coil through my body to demonstrate before a scientific society the comparative harmlessness of very rapidly vibrating electric currents, and I can still recall the astonishment of my audience. I would now undertake, with much less apprehension that I had in that experiment, to transmit through my body with such currents the entire electrical energy of the dynamos now working at Niagara—forty or fifty thousand horse-power. I have produced electrical oscillations which were of such intensity that when circulating through my arms and chest they have melted wires which joined my hands, and still I felt no inconvenience. I have energized with such oscillations a loop of heavy copper wire so powerfully that masses of metal, and even objects of an electrical resistance specifically greater than that of human tissue brought close to or placed within the loop, were heated to a high temperature and melted, often with the violence of an explosion, and yet into this very space in which this terribly-destructive turmoil was going on I have repeatedly thrust my head without feeling anything or experiencing injurious after-effects.

Another observation was that by means of such oscillations light could be produced in a novel and more economical manner, which promised to lead to an ideal system of electric illumination by vacuum-tubes, dispensing with the necessity of renewal of lamps or incandescent filaments, and possibly also with the use of wires in the interior of buildings. The efficiency of this light increases in proportion to the rate of the oscillations, and its commercial success is, therefore, dependent on the economical production of electrical vibrations of transcending rates. In this direction I have met with gratifying success of late, and the practical introduction of this new system of illumination is not far off.

The investigations led to many other valuable observations and results, one of the more important of which was the demonstration of the practicability of supplying electrical energy through one wire without return. At first I was able to transmit in this novel manner only very small amounts of electrical energy, but in this line also my efforts have been rewarded with similar success.

The photograph shown in Fig. 3 illustrates, as its title explains, an actual transmission of this kind effected with apparatus used in other experiments here described. To what a degree the appliances have been perfected since my first demonstrations early in 1891 before a scientific society, when my apparatus was barely capable of lighting one lamp (which result was considered wonderful), will appear when I state that I have now no difficulty in lighting in this manner four or five hundred lamps, and could light many more. In fact, there is no limit to the amount of energy which may in this way be supplied to operate any kind of electrical device.

After demonstrating the practicability of this method of transmission, the thought naturally occurred to me to use the earth as a conductor, thus dispensing with all wires. Whatever electricity may be, it is a fact that it behaves like an incompressible fluid, and the earth may be looked upon as an immense reservoir of electricity, which, I thought, could be disturbed effectively by a properly designed electrical machine. Accordingly, my next efforts were directed toward perfecting a special apparatus which would be highly effective in creating a disturbance of electricity in the earth. The progress in this new direction was necessarily very slow and the work discouraging, until I finally succeeded in perfecting a novel kind of transformer or induction-coil, particularly suited for this special purpose. That it is practicable, in this manner, not only to transmit minute amounts of electrical energy for operating delicate electrical devices, as I contemplated at first, but also electrical energy in appreciable quantities, will appear from an inspection of Fig. 4 (see p. 186), which illustrates an actual experiment of this kind performed with the same apparatus. The result obtained was all the more remarkable as the top end of the coil was not connected to a wire or plate for magnifying the effect.

"WIRELESS" TELEGRAPHY–THE SECRET OF TUNING–ERRORS IN THE HERTZIAN INVESTIGATIONS–A RECEIVER OF WONDERFUL SENSITIVENESS.

As the first valuable result of my experiments in this latter line a system of telegraphy without wires resulted, which I described in two scientific lectures in February and March, 1893. It is mechanically illustrated in diagram *c*, the upper part of which shows the electrical arrangement as I described it then, while the lower part illustrates its mechanical analogue. The system is extremely simple in principle. Imagine two tuning-forks *F*, F_1, one at the sending- and the other at the receiving-station respectively, each having attached to its lower prong a minute piston *p*, fitting in a cylinder. Both the cylinders communicate with a large reservoir *R*, with elastic walls, which is supposed to be closed and filled with a light and incompressible fluid. By striking repeatedly one of the prongs of the tuning-fork *F*, the small piston *p* below would be vibrated, and its vibrations, transmitted through the fluid, would reach the distant fork F_1, which is "tuned" to the fork *F*, or, stated otherwise, of exactly the same note as the latter. The fork F_1 would now be set vibrating, and its vibration would be intensified by the continued action of the distant fork *F* until its upper prong, swinging far out, would make an electrical connection with a stationary contact *c*", starting in this manner some electrical or other appliances which may be used for recording the signals. In this simple way messages could be exchanged between the two stations, a similar contact *c'* being provided for this purpose, close to the upper prong of the fork *F*, so that the apparatus at each station could be employed in turn as receiver and transmitter.

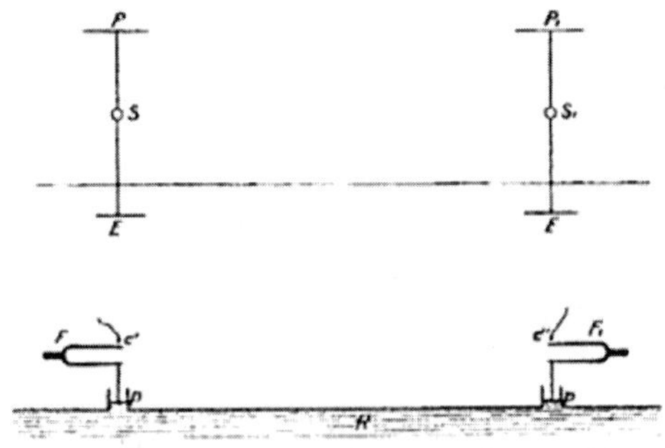

DIAGRAM c. "WIRELESS" TELEGRAPHY MECHANICALLY ILLUSTRATED

The electrical system illustrated in the upper figure of diagram *c* is exactly the same in principle, the two wires or circuits *ESP* and $E_1S_1P_1$, which extend vertically to a height, representing the two tuning-forks with the pistons attached to them. These circuits are connected with the ground by plates *E*, E_1, and to two elevated metal sheets *P*, P_1, which store electricity and thus magnify considerably the effect. The closed reservoir *R*, with elastic walls, is in this case replaced by the earth, and the fluid by electricity. Both of these circuits are "tuned" and operate just like the two tuning-forks. Instead of striking the fork *F* at the sending-station, electrical oscillations are produced in the vertical sending- or transmitting-wire *ESP*, as by the action of a source *S*, included in this wire, which spread through the ground and reach the distant vertical receiving-wire $E_1S_1P_1$, exciting corresponding electrical oscillations in the same. In the latter wire or circuit is included a sensitive device or receiver S_1, which is thus set in action and made to operate a relay or other appliance. Each station is, of course, provided both with a source of electrical oscillations *S* and a sensitive receiver *S1*, and a simple provision is made for using each of the two wires alternately to send and to receive the messages.

The exact attunement of the two circuits secures great advantages, and, in fact, it is essential in the practical use of the system. In this respect many popular errors exist, and, as a rule, in the technical reports on this subject circuits and appliances are described as affording these advantages when from their very nature it is evident that this is impossible. In order to attain the best results it is essential that the length of each wire or circuit, from the ground connection to the top, should be equal to one quarter of the wave-length of the electrical vibration in the wire, or else equal to that length multiplied by an odd number. Without the observation of this rule it is virtually impossible to prevent the interference and insure the privacy of messages. Therein lies the secret of tuning. To obtain the most satisfactory results it is, however, necessary to resort to electrical vibrations of low pitch. The Hertzian spark apparatus, used generally by experimenters, which produces oscillations of a very high rate, permits no effective tuning, and slight disturbances are sufficient to render an exchange of messages impracticable. But scientifically designed, efficient appliances allow nearly perfect adjustment. An experiment performed with the improved apparatus repeatedly referred to, and intended to convey an idea of this feature, is illustrated in Fig. 5, which is sufficiently explained by its note.

Since I described these simple principles of telegraphy without wires I have had frequent occasion to note that the identical features and elements have been used, in the evident belief that the signals are being transmitted to considerable distance by "Hertzian" radiations. This is only one of many misapprehensions to which the investigations of the lamented physicist have given rise. About thirty-three years ago Maxwell, following up a suggestive experiment made by Faraday in 1845, evolved an ideally simple theory which intimately connected light, radiant heat, and electrical phenomena, interpreting them as being all due to vibrations of a hypothetical fluid of inconceivable tenuity, called the ether. No experimental verification was arrived at until Hertz, at the suggestion of Helmholtz, undertook a series of experiments to this effect. Hertz proceeded with extraordinary ingenuity and insight, but devoted little energy to the perfection of his old-fashioned apparatus. The consequence was that he failed to observe the important function which the air played in his experiments, and which I subsequently discovered. Repeating his experiments and reaching different results, I ventured to point out this oversight. The strength of the proofs brought forward by Hertz in support of Maxwell's theory resided in the correct estimate of the rates of vibration of the circuits he used. But I ascertained that he could not have obtained the rates he thought he was getting. The vibrations with identical apparatus he employed are, as a rule, much slower, this being due to the presence of air, which produces a dampening effect upon a rapidly vibrating electric circuit of high pressure, as a fluid does upon a vibrating tuning-fork. I have, however, discovered since that time other causes of error, and I have long ago ceased to look upon his results as being an experimental verification of the poetical conceptions of Maxwell. The work of the great German physicist has acted as an immense stimulus to contemporary electrical research, but it has likewise, in a measure, by its fascination, paralyzed the scientific mind, and thus hampered independent inquiry. Every new phenomenon which was discovered was made to fit the theory, and so very often the truth has been unconsciously distorted.

When I advanced this system of telegraphy, my mind was dominated by the idea of effecting communication to any distance through the earth or environing medium, the practical consummation of which I considered of transcendent importance, chiefly on account of the moral effect which it could not fail to produce universally. As the first effort to this end I proposed at that time, to employ relay-stations with tuned circuits, in the hope of making thus practicable signaling over vast distances, even with apparatus of very moderate power then at my command. I was confident, however, that with properly designed machinery signals could be transmitted to any point of the globe, no matter what the distance, without the necessity of using such intermediate stations. I gained this conviction through the discovery of a singular electrical phenomenon, which I described early in 1892, in lectures I delivered before some scientific societies abroad, and which I have called a "rotating brush." This is a bundle of light which is formed, under certain conditions, in a vacuum-bulb, and which is of a sensitiveness to magnetic and electric influences bordering, so to speak, on the supernatural. This light-bundle is rapidly rotated by the earth's magnetism as many as twenty thousand times pre second, the rotation in these parts being opposite to what it would be in the southern hemisphere, while in the region of the magnetic equator it should not rotate at all. In its most sensitive state, which is difficult to obtain, it is responsive to electric or magnetic influences to an incredible degree. The mere stiffening of the muscles of the arm and consequent slight electrical change in the body of an observer standing at some distance from it, will perceptibly affect it. When in this highly sensitive state it is capable of indicating the slightest magnetic and electric changes taking place in the earth. The observation of this wonderful phenomenon impressed me strongly that communication at any distance could be easily effected by its means, provided that apparatus could be perfected capable of producing an electric or magnetic change of state, however small, in the terrestrial globe or environing medium.

DEVELOPMENT OF A NEW PRINCIPLE–THE ELECTRICAL OSCILLATOR–PRODUCTION OF IMMENSE ELECTRICAL MOVEMENTS–THE EARTH RESPONDS TO MAN–INTERPLANETARY COMMUNICATION NOW PROBABLE.

I resolved to concentrate my efforts upon this venturesome task, though it involved great sacrifice, for the difficulties to be mastered were such that I could hope to consummate it only after years of labor. It meant delay of other work to which I would have preferred to devote myself, but I gained the conviction that my energies could not be more usefully employed; for I recognized that an efficient apparatus for, the production of powerful electrical oscillations, as was needed for that specific purpose, was the key to the solution of other most important electrical and, in fact, human problems. Not only was communication, to any distance, without wires possible by its means, but, likewise, the transmission of energy in great amounts, the burning of the atmospheric nitrogen, the production of an efficient illuminant, and many other results of inestimable scientific and industrial value. Finally, however, I had the satisfaction of accomplishing the task undertaken by the use of a new principle, the virtue of which is based on the marvelous properties of the electrical condenser. One of these is that it can discharge or explode its stored energy in an inconceivably short time. Owing to this it is unequaled in explosive violence. The explosion of dynamite is only the breath of a consumptive compared with its discharge. It is the means of producing the strongest current, the highest electrical pressure, the greatest commotion in the medium. Another of its properties, equally valuable, is that its discharge may vibrate at any rate desired up to many millions per second.

I had arrived at the limit of rates obtainable in other ways when the happy idea presented itself to me to resort to the condenser. I arranged such an instrument so as to be charged and discharged alternately in rapid succession through a coil with a few turns of stout wire, forming the primary of a transformer or induction-coil. Each time the condenser was discharged the current would quiver in the primary wire and induce corresponding oscillations in the secondary. Thus a transformer or induction-coil on new principles was evolved, which I have called "the electrical oscillator," partaking of those unique qualities which characterize the condenser, and enabling results to be attained impossible by other means. Electrical effects of any desired character and of intensities undreamed of before are now easily producible by perfected apparatus of this kind, to which frequent reference has been made, and the essential parts of which are shown in Fig. 6. For certain purposes a strong inductive effect is required; for others the greatest possible suddenness; for others again, an exceptionally high rate of vibration or extreme pressure; while for certain other objects immense electrical movements are necessary. The photographs in Figs. 7, 8, 9, and 10, of experiments performed with such an oscillator, may serve to illustrate some of these features and convey an idea of the magnitude of the effects actually produced. The completeness of the titles of the figures referred to makes a further description of them unnecessary.

However extraordinary the results shown may appear, they are but trifling compared with those which are attainable by apparatus designed on these same principles. I have produced electrical discharges the actual path of which, from end to end, was probably more than one hundred feet long; but it would not be difficult to reach lengths one hundred times as great. I have produced electrical movements occurring at the rate of approximately one hundred thousand horsepower, but rates of one, five, or ten million horse-power are easily practicable. In these experiments effects were developed incomparably greater than any ever produced by human agencies, and yet these results are but an embryo of what is to be.

That communication without wires to any point of the globe is practicable with such apparatus would need no demonstration, but through a discovery which I made I obtained absolute certitude. Popularly explained, it is exactly this: When we raise the voice and hear an echo in reply, we know that the sound of the voice must have reached a distant wall, or boundary, and must have been reflected from the same. Exactly as the sound, so an electrical wave is reflected, and the same evidence which is afforded by an echo is offered by an electrical phenomenon known as a "stationary" wave–that is, a wave with fixed nodal and ventral regions. Instead of sending sound-vibrations toward a distant wall, I have sent electrical vibrations toward the remote boundaries of the earth, and instead of the wall the earth has replied. In place of an echo I have obtained a stationary electrical wave, a wave reflected from afar.

Stationary waves in the earth mean something more than mere telegraphy without wires to any distance. They will enable us to attain many important specific results impossible otherwise. For instance, by their use we may produce at will, from a sending-station, an electrical effect in any particular region of the globe; we may determine the relative position or course of a moving object, such as a vessel at sea, the distance traversed by the same, or its speed; or we may send over the earth a wave of electricity traveling at any rate we desire, from the pace of a turtle up to lightning speed.

With these developments we have every reason to anticipate that in a time not very distant most telegraphic messages across the oceans will be transmitted without cables. For short distances we need a "wireless" telephone, which requires no expert operators. The greater the spaces to be bridged, the more rational becomes communication without wires. The cable is not only an easily damaged and costly instrument, but it limits us in the speed of transmission by reason of a certain electrical property inseparable from its construction. A properly designed plant for effecting communication without wires ought to have many times the working capacity of a cable, while it will involve incomparably less expense. Not a long time will pass, I believe, before communication by cable will become obsolete, for not only will signaling by this new method be quicker and cheaper, but also much safer. By using some new means for isolating the messages which I have contrived, an almost perfect privacy can be secured.

I have observed the above effects so far only up to a limited distance of about six hundred miles, but inasmuch as there is virtually no limit to the power of the vibrations producible with such an oscillator, I feel quite confident of the success of such a plant for effecting transoceanic communication. Nor is this all. My measurements and calculations have shown that it is perfectly practicable to produce on our globe, by the use of these principles, an electrical movement of such magnitude that, without the slightest doubt, its effect will be perceptible on some of our nearer planets, as Venus and Mars. Thus from mere possibility interplanetary communication has entered the stage of probability. In fact, that we can produce a distinct effect on one of these planets in this novel manner, namely, by disturbing the electrical condition of the earth, is beyond any doubt. This way of effecting such communication is, however, essentially different from all others which have so far been proposed by scientific men. In all the previous instances only a minute fraction of the total energy reaching the planet–as much as it would be possible to concentrate in a reflector–could be utilized by the supposed observer in his instrument. But by the means I have developed he would be enabled to concentrate the larger portion of the entire energy transmitted to the planet in his instrument, and the chances of affecting the latter are thereby increased many millionfold.

Besides machinery for producing vibrations of the required power, we must have delicate means capable of revealing the effects of feeble influences exerted upon the earth. For such purposes, too, I have perfected new methods. By their use we shall likewise be able, among other things, to detect at considerable distance the presence of an iceberg or other object at sea. By their use, also, I have discovered some terrestrial phenomena still unexplained. That we can send a message to a planet is certain, that we can get an answer is probable: man is not the only being in the Infinite gifted with a mind.

TRANSMISSION OF ELECTRICAL ENERGY TO ANY DISTANCE WITHOUT WIRES–NOW PRACTICABLE–THE BEST MEANS OF INCREASING THE FORCE ACCELERATING THE HUMAN MASS.

The most valuable observation made in the course of these investigations was the extraordinary behavior of the atmosphere toward electric impulses of excessive electromotive force. The experiments showed that the air at the ordinary pressure became distinctly conducting, and this opened up the wonderful prospect of transmitting large amounts of electrical energy for industrial purposes to great distances without wires, a possibility which, up to that time, was thought of only as a scientific dream. Further investigation revealed the important fact that the conductivity imparted to the air by these electrical impulses of many millions of volts increased very rapidly with the degree of rarefaction, so that air strata at very moderate altitudes, which are easily accessible, offer, to all experimental evidence, a perfect conducting path, better than a copper wire, for currents of this character.

Thus the discovery of these new properties of the atmosphere not only opened up the possibility of transmitting, without wires, energy in large amounts, but, what was still more significant, it afforded the certitude that energy could be transmitted in this manner economically. In this new system it matters little–in fact, almost nothing–whether the transmission is effected at a distance of a few miles or of a few thousand miles.

While I have not, as yet, actually effected a transmission of a considerable amount of energy, such as would be of industrial importance, to a great distance by this new method, I have operated several model plants under exactly the same conditions which will exist in a large plant of this kind, and the practicability of the system is thoroughly demonstrated. The experiments have shown conclusively that, with two terminals maintained at an elevation of not more than thirty thousand to thirty-five thousand feet above sea-level, and with an electrical pressure of fifteen to twenty million volts, the energy of thousands of horse-power can be transmitted over distances which may be hundreds and, if necessary, thousands of miles. I am hopeful, however, that I may be able to reduce very considerably the elevation of the terminals now required, and with this object I am following up an idea which promises such a realization. There is, of course, a popular prejudice against using an electrical pressure of millions of volts, which may cause sparks to fly at distances of hundreds of feet, but, paradoxical as it may seem, the system, as I have described it in a technical publication, offers greater personal safety than most of the ordinary distribution circuits now used in the cities. This is, in a measure, borne out by the fact that, although I have carried on such experiments for a number of years, no injury has been sustained either by me or any of my assistants.

But to enable a practical introduction of the system, a number of essential requirements are still to be fulfilled. It is not enough to develop appliances by means of which such a transmission can be effected. The machinery must be such as to allow the transformation and transmission, of electrical energy under highly economic and practical conditions. Furthermore, an inducement must be offered to those who are engaged in the industrial exploitation of natural sources of power, as waterfalls, by guaranteeing greater returns on the capital invested than they can secure by local development of the property.

From that moment when it was observed that, contrary to the established opinion, low and easily accessible strata of the atmosphere are capable of conducting electricity, the transmission of electrical energy without wires has become a rational task of the engineer, and one surpassing all others in importance. Its practical consummation would mean that energy would be available for the uses of man at any point of the globe, not in small amounts such as might be derived from the ambient medium by suitable machinery, but in quantities virtually unlimited, from waterfalls. Export of power would then become the chief source of income for many happily situated countries, as the United States, Canada, Central and South America, Switzerland, and Sweden. Men could settle down everywhere, fertilize and irrigate the soil with little effort, and convert barren deserts into gardens, and thus the entire globe could be transformed and made a fitter abode for mankind. It is highly probable that if there are intelligent beings on Mars they have long ago realized this very idea, which would explain the changes on its surface noted by astronomers. The atmosphere on that planet, being of considerably smaller density than that of the earth, would make the task much more easy.

It is probable that we shall soon have a self-acting heat-engine capable of deriving moderate amounts of energy from the ambient medium. There is also a possibility–though a small one–that we may obtain electrical energy direct from the sun. This might be the case if the Maxwellian theory is true, according to which electrical vibrations of all rates should emanate from the sun. I am still investigating this subject. Sir William Crookes has shown in his beautiful invention known as the "radiometer" that rays may produce by impact a mechanical effect, and this may lead to some important revelation as to the utilization of the sun's rays in novel ways. Other sources of energy may be opened up, and new methods of deriving energy from the sun discovered, but none of these or similar achievements would equal in importance the transmission of power to any distance through the medium. I can conceive of no technical advance which would tend to unite the various elements of humanity more effectively than this one, or of one which would more add to and more economize human energy. It would be the best means of increasing the force accelerating the human mass. The mere moral influence of such a radical departure would be incalculable. On the other hand if at any point of the globe energy can be obtained in limited quantities from the ambient medium by means of a self-acting heat-engine or otherwise, the conditions will remain the same as before. Human performance will be increased, but men will remain strangers as they were.

I anticipate that any, unprepared for these results, which, through long familiarity, appear to me simple and obvious, will consider them still far from practical application. Such reserve, and even opposition, of some is as useful a quality and as necessary an element in human progress as the quick receptivity and enthusiasm of others. Thus, a mass which resists the force at first, once set in movement, adds to the energy. The scientific man does not aim at an immediate result. He does not expect that his advanced ideas will be readily taken up. His work is like that of the planter–for the future. His duty is to lay the foundation for those who are to come, and point the way. He lives and labors and hopes with the poet who says:

Schaff' das Tagwerk meiner Hande,
Hohes Gluck, dass ich's vollende!
Lass, o lass mich nicht ermatten!
Nein, es sind nicht leere Traume:
Jetzt nur Stangen, diese Baume
Geben einst noch Frucht und Schatten.[1]

---

1. Daily work–my hands' employment,
To complete is pure enjoyment!
Let, oh, let me never falter!
No! there is no empty dreaming:
Lo! these trees, but bare poles seeming,
Yet will yield both food and shelter!
Goethe's "Hope"
Translated by William Gibson, Com. U. S. N.